COWBOYS & KISSES

LENOX RANCH COWBOYS - BOOK 1

VANESSA VALE

Cover design: Bridger Media

Cover Photos: Wander Aguiar Photography; Deposit Photos: Photocreo

This book was previously published as Rose in the Wildflower Brides Series.

GET A FREE BOOK!

Join my mailing list to be the first to know of new releases, free books, special prices and other author giveaways.

http://freeromanceread.com

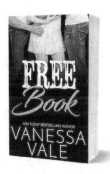

1

OSE

THE KITCHEN at six in the morning was akin to what I remembered of busy Chicago intersections—crowded, loud and slightly dangerous. With ten women in the house, there was never quiet, never any peace. It was the same, day in and day out. Dahlia bickered with Miss Esther about how the bacon should be cooked. Poppy stood behind Lily and styled her blond hair in another inventive creation. Marigold set the table with a loud clatter of dishes, eager for her meal. Hyacinth sat at the large table humming placidly to herself as she sewed on a button. Iris and Daisy were most likely still asleep or at least taking their time in dressing as to avoid morning chores. I paused and watched the hubbub, shaking my head at the claustrophobic feel in the room.

Nothing had changed. The room had not changed

since the first day we'd all arrived from Chicago sixteen years before. Besides being older, *no one* had changed; our personalities were as varied as ever. Except me. *I'd* changed. Why did everyone irk me? Why did the house suddenly seem so small? Why did my sisters seem so grating? Why did I feel like I was being suffocated?

Wanting to escape, I dropped the armful of wood into the bin beside the stove and walked right back outside, and started across the grass to the stable. I took deep breaths of the cool morning air in an attempt to settle myself. It was too early to be riled, especially from just the normal morning routine.

"Rose!" Miss Trudy's voice carried all the way to me. There was more than physical distance between us; there was an emotional separation as well. I stopped and turned back with a sigh, tucking my unruly hair behind my ear. The woman who'd raised eight orphan girls, myself included, held up a folded cloth. "If you won't eat at the table, at least take something with you."

Her hair was up in a simple bun at her nape of her neck, the gray in her red hair bright in the sun just breaking over the mountains. She was still beautiful, even with the fine lines that showed her age. As I mounted the steps to take the food, I saw concern in her green eyes, but refused to speak of it.

I smelled the biscuits and bacon and my stomach rumbled. "Thanks," I replied, with a semblance of a smile on my lips.

"Where will you be?" she asked, her voice calm and placid. She never shouted, never raised her voice.

No one went off without sharing their whereabouts,

for dangers abounded the ranch and all of Montana Territory beyond.

"I'll follow the fence line to look for any sections that might need repair." There was no damaged fence line. I knew it and so did Miss Trudy, but she only gave a small nod, allowing me to escape.

Not sure what else to say, I turned to head towards the stable. I couldn't tell her I was unhappy, although I was sure she knew. Uttering the words would make me seem ungrateful. She and Miss Esther had provided a stable, loving home for all of us girls. I would have grown up in a large city, never knowing the open expanses and big sky of Montana if they hadn't claimed us all and brought us west. The thought had me rubbing the space above my heart, guilt and a restlessness pressing heavily. No matter the depth of her caring or the closeness I had with the other girls, I needed more. I needed to escape.

———

"WHATEVER THAT FENCE post did to you, it sure is sorry now."

The deep voice that came from behind me was such a surprise that I hit my thumb with the hammer. I was a mile from the house when I'd decided to work out some of my frustrations on the fence. The post had had a loose nail and I'd begun to pound it in, continuing to strike even after it was lodged back in the wood. I was still hammering when he caught me unawares.

I sucked in a breath at the searing pain in the tip of my thumb, holding the base of it in my other hand. I let a few less-than-ladylike words slip out as I winced, walking around in a circle.

"Chance Goodman!" I shouted, my anger and pain loud and clear. "You don't sneak up on someone like that."

The man was ten years older than I and lived on the nearest ranch. His parents had died a few years earlier and with much success, he'd taken over the spread, adding more cattle and even studding out his prized bulls. The latter made me flush every time I thought of it, for I knew what happened between a man and a woman —Miss Trudy and Miss Esther were former brothel owners and had given each of us girls a special talk—and I'd always pictured Chance's face in my mind when I imagined such acts. I'd seen one of his bulls and the...the thing that hung down from beneath its belly and it had me wondering what Chance would look like. Would he be large himself? Would he be just as aggressive when he mounted a woman? My nipples always tightened into hard points and I felt slickness between my legs every time I imagined such a scenario.

There was no other man for fifty miles who was so fine a specimen of manhood as Chance Goodman. I'd thought so when I was nine, and I thought the same now at nineteen. His hair was a chocolate brown which he let run toward the overly long. He towered over me; I only came up to his shoulder and made me feel...feminine. There were eight women in the house who cared about ribbons and lace when I was more interested in saddle leather and branding. But Chance often made me wish I'd combed my hair or worn clothing that made me appear more comely, at least in his eyes.

It wasn't his broad shoulders or thickly corded forearms that had my heart pounding whenever I saw him. It wasn't the way a dimple dented his cheek whenever he smiled. It wasn't the strong jaw nor the big hands so much as his dark eyes that attracted me. He was the only person who passed whatever facade I raised to hide my true self. It was as if I were constantly exposed, every emotion and feeling I had was clear as spring water to him. I couldn't hide from him, even when, like now, he stood right before me.

"Here, let me see." He took my hand as I turned toward him. Before I could step away, he lifted it up so he could look at it, then, to my complete and utter surprise, slipped my injured thumb into his mouth. My own mouth fell open in utter surprise. My thumb was in Chance Goodman's mouth...and it felt good. His tongue flicked over the injured tip, sucking on it as if withdrawing the pain as he would venom from a snakebite. His mouth was hot and wet and my finger pulsed—among other places—and it wasn't from the hammer.

"What...what are you doing?" I asked, my words tumbling out in a confused rush. Chance had never even touched me before. He'd given me his linked palms to use as a step to mount a horse, but that was nothing compared to this. The way his dark eyes captured mine as his tongue flicked over my thumb was new. Gentle, possessive, *hot*. God, this was the most carnal thing I'd ever experienced and it was just my thumb! What would happen to me if he took even greater liberties?

At that enticing and very scary thought, I tugged my

hand back. He could easily have kept it, for his strength was so much greater than mine, but he released me of his own choosing.

"Better?" he asked. His voice was deep and rough, reminding me of stones in the river.

I could only nod in response, as I was still flustered.

"I think this is the first time I've made you speechless." The corner of his mouth turned up and his dimple appeared.

I put my hands on my hips, ignoring the pain. "What do you want?" I asked, my tone acerbic.

His gaze raked over my body, assessing. He sighed. "Right now? I want to know what's wrong."

"Besides my thumb?" I held my hand up. "Nothing," I grumbled.

"Rose," he said, his voice raised in that irritating warning tone.

"What? Can't a girl have some secrets?"

His dark eyebrows went up. "Since when do you consider yourself a girl?" He glanced down at the pants I wore instead of the skirt or dress of every other female. The barb stung, for it only validated my earlier insecurities. He didn't think of me as a woman. He thought of me as...Rose. Plain Rose in pants. What man could ever be interested in a woman who'd rather wear pants than ribbons and lace? What man could desire a woman who hammered fence posts?

"Since...." I clamped my mouth shut. "Oh, bother." I turned away from him and stomped off.

"Is Dahlia pestering you again?" he called out. "Or did Marigold eat your breakfast?"

I knew he was toying with me, for he'd never poke fun at the other girls. He was too much of a gentleman. It didn't keep him from poking fun at *me*. When Miss Trudy and Miss Esther found us girls, orphaned after the great Chicago fire, they hadn't known our names. Why they gave us all names of flowers, I'll never know. Moving to the Montana Territory had been a way for all of us to start over, especially Miss Trudy and Miss Esther. Well off from their years running a big city brothel, they'd wanted a new life and found it outside the town of Clayton. We were infamously known as the Montana wildflowers and were always considered as a group of eight, not as individuals.

"Everyone is the same. *Nothing's* changed."

"Are you wanting something different then?" He leaned a hip against the battered fence post, relaxed and at ease with himself while offering me his complete attention. I saw his horse in the distance, head lowered and nibbling grass. A bird flew overhead, its wings still as it rode a wind current.

"Something different? Of course I want something different!" I waved my arms in the air as I spoke. "I want to be independent, wild. Free! Not stuck in a house full of women who gab all day long about hairstyles and dress sleeve length. I want to do what Miss Trudy did—strike out and discover a whole new life in a far off land."

He patiently let me vent my spleen. "What do you plan to do?"

"I don't know, Chance, but I'm about to burst out of my own skin. Don't you see? I don't belong anymore." I lowered my head with that admission, for I felt shame and guilt press heavily on my heart. Miss Trudy and Miss Esther had done so much for me, for all of the girls, and I was tossing all those years, all the love aside. I pressed once again to that spot on my chest as I felt tears well. Lifting my head to the sky, I sniffed and forced the tears back. I didn't cry. I *never* cried and I was mad at Chance for making me feel this way.

With his long stride, he walked toward me through the tall grass and tilted my chin up with his fingers, forcing me to look at him. My hat fell off my head to dangle by the long cord around my neck. His scent, a mixture of warm skin and pine and leather was something I associated solely with him. "No. You don't belong here anymore."

I couldn't believe that he agreed with me. The one person who I expected to fight for me—my friend— agreed with me. He wanted me to leave. I tore my chin from his hold and stomped over to my horse, quickly mounting. Using the reins to turn the animal, I gave Chance Goodman one last look. It was time to move on; he'd just confirmed that for me. My heart hurt, knowing I'd never see him again. I settled my hat back on my head, gave it a little flick with my finger in farewell and rode off. Not only did the tip of my thumb ache, but also my heart.

2

ROSE

THE SKY WAS black as pitch, just as dark in Clayton as it was on the ranch. Only lanterns shining from a few houses lit the way. I'd left my horse at the livery and made my way toward the boarding house. The night was warm so I didn't need a shawl or a coat, and only carried a small bag. I would take the next stage out of town, not caring whether it ventured east or west. Clayton wasn't large, but the livery was across town from where I would spend the night, forcing me to walk the distance alone. It wasn't the best choice considering the kinds of men that passed through town, but there was no alternative. Mines abounded up in the mountains and Clayton had the nearest saloon. This meant whiskey and women. It was one of these men who I unfortunately encountered on my way.

I walked quickly with my small bag over my shoulder, but the man had caught me unawares, stepping from between two buildings and into my path. I'd been thinking about Chance and our parting words. I didn't have a gun or a knife or any kind of weapon to protect myself when I walked directly into him with an *oomph*. I couldn't see his face in the dark but distinct body odor of sweat and whiskey emanated from his pores. His hands were quick and grabbed me about the arms.

"Look what I've captured! A lady of the night."

"I beg your pardon! I do not look anything like a lady of the night," I replied, offended. Despite my being unladylike, I did not deserve the comparison. I fought against his hold, a burst of energy making my heart beat swiftly. "Unhand me!" I cried.

"Oh, no. You're mine now." He roughly spun me around so that one of his arms banded about my waist in a viselike grip, making it difficult to breathe. His hold was strong enough where he lifted me up so only the tips of my toes touched the ground. The other hand went over my mouth, grimy fingers preventing me from screaming. I knew this because I tried, yet it only made him rougher in his manhandling. I was dragged into an alley, then behind a building. The hand came from my mouth for a moment to open a door, only to return it and squelch another scream. Using a foot, he kicked the door shut behind him, making the cheap windows rattle. I could hear a tinny piano playing and the air was heavy with the smell of whiskey—not just from my abductor—and thick cigar smoke.

A man scrubbing dishes in a deep pump sink turned

his head and paused, plate in hand. I made sounds against the palm over my mouth, my eyes wide, pleading for him to help me, but he just turned back and continued his task. A narrow wooden stairway led upwards and the man turned sideways so we could both fit as he climbed, bumping me into the rough-hewn wall.

At the top, he released me, my feet touching the ground and air entering my lungs. I could see the top of a second stairwell at the far end of the hall, the music louder from here. A woman—who most certainly was a lady of the night—stood scantily clad speaking with a man who seemed quite pleased with her forward attentions. Further along were two men who leaned over a railing, presumably to view the saloon downstairs. I had no doubt as to my whereabouts; the establishment had been just down the street from where the man grabbed me and it was easy to infer from the men, the woman and the liquor.

"You can scream, but no one will help." The man leaned down to speak directly into my ear. His breath was hot and fetid. "They'll think you're playing, that you like it rough. I do. I like it when a woman fights."

A bitter taste filled my mouth at his unpalatable words. My only consideration was preventing this man from pulling me into one of the many rooms that lined the hall. From Miss Trudy and Miss Esther's tales, I knew what occurred in the upstairs of a saloon, and it wasn't for me. Screaming and running off might not bring me the help I wanted, for someone might just drag me right back to the man or take liberties himself. I had to defend myself!

I remembered what Miss Esther had taught us about fending off an overeager suitor. This man most certainly wasn't a suitor, but he more than qualified. I raised my knee and stomped down onto the top of his foot with all my might. He had heavy leather boots that softened the blow, but it surprised him enough to loosen his grip. I rammed my elbow backward, directly into his man parts.

A muffled, high-pitched groan came from between his clenched teeth.

His hands went to cover his injury and I didn't delay. I dashed down the hall in the direction of the front stairwell.

"I'll get you, bitch."

At his hissed warning, I turned my head to look back at the dastardly man, which prevented me from seeing the man who stepped into my path. I ran solidly into him with my shoulder and my head. Once again, strong arms banded about me.

"No. Let me go!" I fought him with a burst of energy founded in fear.

"Rose. Stop." The voice was familiar, but that wasn't what had me stilling. It was his scent that I recognized. *Chance.*

I settled immediately and looked up at my friend, my savior. I didn't see the friendliness or warmth I usually saw there. Instead, his eyes were narrowed, his jaw clenched tightly and a tick pulsed in his cheek. He was more warrior than cowboy. "Did he hurt you?"

His dark gaze raked over my face, then my body as he pushed me away from him. He didn't release me, keeping a firm grip on my shoulders. This time, I did not mind a man's hands upon my person, nor his roving stare. Besides the odd thumb incident earlier in the day, it was the only time he'd touched me. His hands were quite large and very warm. The solid weight of his grip was comforting instead of confining.

My assailant had recovered somewhat and made his way over to us, back stooped. "She belongs to me." The fury that coated his words made his tone even more petrifying than before. I knew now that if he were alone with me, being raped would be the least of my concerns. He had a cloak of menacing danger about him that had me stumbling back a step and against Chance's solid body.

"I believe the woman disagrees," Chance countered.

I nodded my head vehemently, hair falling in my face. I tucked it back behind my ear.

The other man wiped his mouth with his fingers as he stared at me. "Doesn't matter. She was out on the street flaunting her...attributes." His gaze lowered and I shivered, knowing he was thinking carnal thoughts about me.

"I did no such thing," I replied, my voice laced with indignation.

"If she did as you said, then I assure you that she will be readily punished for her behavior. My...wife is not right in the head."

I turned to look up at Chance. The man shifted his attention as well.

"Wife?" we said in unison.

What kind of lie was Chance perpetrating? I was most certainly *not* his wife.

"I think we can agree that this little incident never happened. I don't need word about my wife spread any more than people want to know you abducted a lady. But if I so much as see your face again, I'll haul your ass to the sheriff only after I beat the stuffing out of you." Chance's words held bite and the other man knew it. He took a step back, recognizing his evening plans had quickly changed.

"If she's as crazy as you say, you should keep a closer watch on her, mister." He pointed at me as he retreated. "She could come across someone with less savory attentions in mind."

The irony of the man's words was not lost on Chance. He pushed me behind him and stepped toward my assailant, fists clenched. The man knew his time to leave had come, and I watched around Chance's broad torso as he fled the way we'd come, his footfall heavy on the back stairs.

Only the sounds of the piano music and voices filtered up from the saloon below. The hallway was deserted now. My heartbeat was loud in my ears, my breathing fast.

Chance turned and faced me, hands on hips. I wasn't just thankful that he'd saved me. Thrilled, even. But I was also embarrassed at being caught in such a compromising, weak position. I had been able to take care of myself on the ranch, but only a few minutes in town alone and I needed a rescuer.

I was also angry, and angry hid humiliation very well. "Why did you say that about me?"

His eyes narrowed into slits. "The only way the Rose

Lenox I know would do something so utterly stupid is if she were not right in the head."

Gone was my longtime friend. In his place was a man I didn't recognize—intense, bold and very, very virile. I'd always seen Chance as a man, but not a *man*. This was different. *He* was different. Although his ire was directed solely at me, I couldn't help but appreciate this new iteration of Chance Goodman.

"I think there's something wrong with you. You told the man I was your wife!"

His brows went up and he grinned, showing me a flash of straight white teeth and his dangerous dimple. "I did." When I continued to just glower at him, he continued. "He wouldn't have just handed you over to me, especially since you practically unmanned him. I had to claim you."

"You did not have to do any such thing. Dragging me bodily from the building would have been sufficient."

"Don't worry, I still intend to do that," he vouched. "Let's go."

He took my arm and led me down the stairs, across the saloon and out into the dark night. I kept my head down and remained as close to Chance's side, having no interest in remaining within a moment longer. The air was cool and fresh and I was relieved that he'd saved me. I knew how close I'd come to a dire situation and I would thank the man readily enough, but I was still fuming over his tactic. I was not his wife, nor remotely insane.

I was lost in my thoughts and only realized we'd stopped when Chance knocked on a door to a small house. Looking around, I noticed we were just off the main thoroughfare beside the jail. After a moment, the door opened.

"Good evening, Sheriff," Chance said to the man, removing his hat.

Sheriff! "You're going to have me arrested? You are the one not right in the head, Chance Goodman!" I stepped back from him, shaking my head.

The sheriff stepped out of the doorway, the soft yellow light from inside his small home illuminating the three of us.

"I should have you thrown in jail for your own protection, but no. No jail for you," Chance replied.

"Miss." The sheriff nodded his head in my direction, and then looked to Chance. "Goodman, it's been a long time. What can I do for you?"

"I'm in need of your services," Chance replied. He was going to have me arrested. The gall of the man! "As Justice Of The Peace."

I froze at his words. Justice Of The....

The sheriff grinned.

I frowned. "You *really* want to marry me?" I pointed at Chance. "It was just an excuse to get out of that bad environment."

"Bad environment?" He shook his head, taking a moment. "You were on the second floor of the saloon, Rose, with a man who had plans for your person that were less than consensual." Chance shook his head slowly, his eyes on me. "Oh, no. You need a keeper, and as I told the bastard you would be punished. I don't have any right to punish you, Rose, unless you're my wife."

"You're going to beat me?" I countered. "Sheriff, did you hear that? He's going to beat me."

The older man's hands went out in front of him in surrender, but remained quiet.

"I'm not going to beat you," Chance replied with a weary sigh, took his hat off and ran his hand through his unruly hair. "I protect what's mine. You're mine, Rose. Always have been. I'll even protect you from yourself."

My mouth fell open. *You're mine, Rose. Always have been.* Those words spun around in my brain making me dizzy.

"Let's get this done, Sheriff."

3

HANCE

"LET'S GET THIS DONE?" Rose repeated, her voice full of sarcasm and surprise. The little hellcat was just getting started. I stifled a grin, knowing it would only build her ire to a fevered pitch if she saw it, but I loved her spirit. That spirit, however, put her into a heap of trouble. I didn't know if I wanted to strangle her or kiss her. The stupid, beautiful woman had no sense, venturing alone at night. Of course, a man would grab her and want to have his way with her.

I wanted to. I'd wanted to for far longer than I should have, but I'd bided my time. At least my intentions were honorable. I hadn't even touched her until today. I'd kept my distance, afraid I'd do something rash like kiss her if she were within reach. Earlier, when she'd hurt her thumb, all I wanted to do was take her hurt away; I didn't even think about my actions until I had the soft tip of her thumb in my mouth. It was the most erotic thing I'd ever done. Seeing the look of surprise and...desire flare in her eyes had my resolution to be patient crumbling. I was resolute now in another way. I would have her; I would make her mine. I would keep her safe. If I could only get her to agree to the damn marriage then I could ensure that. Until then, she would go about wild and untamed, a danger to herself.

"You didn't even ask me!" she shouted. She was so small next to me, petite and dainty, but she was far from it. Feisty, spirited, uninhibited would be more apt.

"You didn't stick around the ranch long enough for me to do so," I countered.

The sheriff chuckled and mumbled something about a hotheaded couple, but we ignored him.

She looked taken aback, as if she hadn't known I would ask her. Perhaps I'd been too successful in hiding my interest.

"I...I didn't know," she replied, her voice soft.

"Of course, you didn't. You're too young."

"I'm nineteen!" She paced around in a circle and I watched her, enjoying the sight of her in a skirt and blouse—unusual attire for her. Her hair had been in a bun at the nape of her neck but the pins had fallen out, leaving the curly blond locks wild down her back. She tucked some wayward strands behind her ear absently. I'd never seen it unbound, for it was always tucked beneath her hat or in a thick plait down her back. The sight of it long and free-flowing was something intimate for only a spouse to see. I saw it as a sign that she was to be mine. It made me want to tangle my fingers in it, wrap the tresses around my hand and tilt her head back so I could kiss her. Claim her mouth and very soon, claim her body.

"I came to Clayton to ask you, but then when I found you with *that man,* I had to save you from getting yourself hurt."

"You followed me." She hadn't stated it as a question.

I ran my hand through my hair, and then stopped her pacing with a hand on her biceps so she'd look at me. "I've always followed you, Rose. Always will."

"But you said—" She bit her bottom lip.

I frowned. "Said what?"

"Earlier, when I was mending fences, you said I didn't belong on the ranch anymore."

Shaking my head, I slowly pulled her closer. "No, *you* said you didn't belong on the ranch anymore, and I agreed."

"Same difference," she muttered, not meeting my eye anymore. "Then why didn't you let me go?"

"You don't belong on the Lenox ranch anymore, kitten. You're being stifled there. You know it and I can see it. I've seen it for a stretch now, but earlier, I knew you'd decided it was time to move on. You belong with me on the Goodman spread. As a Goodman, Rose Goodman."

Her green eyes widened. "You mean...I thought—"

I put my finger over lips. "You thought wrong."

The sheriff cleared his throat. "This is touching and all, but are you needing my services or not?"

"Well?" I asked. "Rose Lenox, will you marry me?"

"WHY ARE we riding back to your ranch when we could stay at the boarding house?" Rose asked.

It was late, well past midnight, but the moon had risen and our path was bright. The ride was only an hour to the ranch house, but it seemed to be interminable. With the vows said, the chaste kiss shared, and the sheriff once again reading his book, I was in a hurry to get my wife home. She sat sideways upon my lap, her ass shifting with the motion of the horse making my mind distracted and my cock very eager. The only thing preventing me from claiming her was the distance from our current location and my bed.

"I don't want to have an audience for our wedding night." I shifted, my cock aching and uncomfortable in my pants.

"Audience? I had my own room."

The corner of my mouth ticked up at her innocence. "I'm going to make you scream your pleasure, kitten, and I guarantee everyone would have heard."

"Oh," she murmured, shifting in my lap some more. She was secure within my hold, my arms around her as I held the reins, her head tucked beneath my chin. Her scent was soft and familiar to me, but having her so close had the floral scent surround me. Somehow, she smelled just like her name. All of her adopted sisters were named after flowers and Rose wasn't even the oldest. Marigold was. Yet Rose was the first to marry.

"You tricked me, you know," she said as we climbed a

small ridge. There were mountains in the distance to the west, but it was not bright enough to discern them.

"Tricked you?" I may have followed her to Clayton, even applied a little coercion to wed, but she wanted the union as much as I. She just hadn't had time to consider and accept it.

Femininity was not something she flaunted. If a man saw past her tomboyish ways and came calling or expressed the slightest interest, Rose directed him toward one of her sisters. She wore pants and usually had pieces of hay caught in her hair. I was the only man she'd allowed into her life, the only man she told her secrets to. The only man who wanted her just as she was, all prickly exterior hiding a most passionate interior, was me. I'd been ready since the day she turned eighteen. Hell, even then I'd waited another seventeen months. 'Tricked' would not be the word I'd use. 'Patient,' just or 'ready' would all be more apt.

"You told that awful man I was your wife. You didn't need to do that and now look at me."

I couldn't see her well from my position, but I could feel her. Smell her. Ache for her. Her hips were slim, yet I could feel her lush curves nonetheless.

"You let yourself fall victim to a lecherous man with no moral leanings," I countered. I wouldn't kowtow to her.

She was perturbed that we'd wed, but she was sore about something else, and it wasn't that I'd told the bastard a lie. I just had to be patient enough to find out what it was, which was going to be a hard task. My patience with her was at an end.

"This wasn't my plan, Chance. You took away my plan!" She waved her hands as she spoke, bumping into my arms.

Ah, now we were at the crux of her frustrations.

"I took away your plans? You *ran* away, like a child!" I took a breath. "What, pray tell, were your plans?"

I'd listened to her like this for years. Heard her woes since she was a little thing. A pet chicken that had ended up in a soup pot. A skinned knee falling from a tree. A boy from town who'd dipped her braid in ink. A rope swing that was used to cross a creek instead of a bridge. An interest in running her own ranch. As time went on, her problems and plans changed, from simple to sophisticated, from childlike to mature. All the while I'd listened without offering any advice, or help. Until today.

While she lived in a loving home, it was crowded, and the other members of the female household frowned on what they considered Rose's manly pursuits. Her ideas were stifled. *She* was stifled, but she'd never done anything reckless enough to endanger herself before.

"I was going to take the next stage out of town. East or west, it didn't matter. I just needed to be gone."

The idea that she would venture alone without a plan or direction had my palm twitching. She needed to be taken in hand before she hurt herself and I wasn't there to save her.

"With just the clothes on your back? How much money do you have?"

"Fifty-six dollars."

I ran my chin back and forth gently over the top of her head, enjoying the silky feel of her hair. The action may have seemed gentle and comforting to Rose, but I did it as a way to stall my words, to allow me a moment to get my frustration to a manageable level so I could speak with a calm voice.

"The man at the saloon, I'm guessing he was offering you aid in your adventure?" I asked, my tone quite sarcastic. The very idea of that man's hands on her had my jaw clenching.

"He was an...unexpected impediment."

I couldn't help but grunt at that understatement.

"I know what you're thinking," she replied.

No, I doubted she did, for my thoughts veered to her either over my knee with her ass turning nice and pink or naked and her mouth occupied around my cock.

"Oh?" My voice had a noticeable growl to it.

"That I was impetuous."

"I have been aware of that for quite some time," I countered dryly. Nothing she'd said about her foray into freedom told me to the contrary. "Are you remotely aware of the things he was going to do to you?"

"I live with two former brothel owners," she countered, as if this made her an expert.

"Those *things* he was going to take belong to *me,* Rose. Me! Your maidenhead is mine. Your body is mine!"

She squirmed against my hold. "Let me go, Chance." Sitting sideways as she was, she dexterously worked her way out from the circle of my arms and slid off the horse. Any other woman would have landed unceremoniously on her ass, but Rose was an accomplished equestrian and landed on her feet readily enough and walked off, arms folded over her chest. I halted the motion of the horse and dismounted, letting the reins drop so the animal could eat the tall grass.

Rose was as prickly as the flower bearing her name. I had to learn not to goad her, especially when she was riled. I wanted her beneath me, not walking away. I needed to know, however, what her intentions were. Leaving town without a plan indicated desperation over forethought. Now that she was mine, this impetuousness would be curbed, her recklessness would be curtailed, or she would be punished. I could not have her hurt.

And so I was in a conundrum. She needed a gentle touch while at the same time a firm, guiding hand. I had to learn to curb her reckless ways while allowing her to bloom. She needed to bend in her *plans*, yet still flourish. All she had to do was let go and I'd catch her. She just didn't understand. It was going to be a battle of wills, but in the interim, there was one way we could be equals and I would show her readily enough. Once I got my hands on her....

"Rose," I called. "You're my wife now. I'll never let you go."

"I wanted to be free!" She paused, her shape amorphous and ghostly beneath the moonlight.

"Free? Free? Alone and vulnerable is *not* free! You almost paid the price tonight with that bastard."

"I was going to run my own ranch somewhere. Statehood's coming and I want to be known as having the best one in all of Montana."

"By yourself? Even on the Lenox land you have Big Ed to help."

I spoke to her back and waited for her to turn. One

word and I'd have her spinning to face me, yet she'd be full of spit and vinegar. I had to proceed carefully, slowly, as if she were a mare ready to breed: skittish yet excited, nervous yet feisty.

"I don't need any help." Her words were clear, but her conviction was waning. "I'm good at running a ranch."

"With no land? No stock? You're a Goodman now and you'll help me run mine. Ours. You don't have to go it alone, kitten."

She spun around, walked up to me and poked me in the chest. "I am *not* your kitten."

4

 HANCE

I GRABBED her hand and pressed it against my chest as I curled my other palm around the nape of her neck. I nudged my hat off so it fell to the ground as I lowered my head and pulled her in for a kiss. This wasn't the chaste touching of lips from the wedding ceremony. This...*this*...was what I'd dreamed of, waited for. Her lips were plump and soft and when she parted them to gasp, I took the opportunity to delve deep. My tongue plundered her mouth, tasting her for the first time. The fist pressed against my chest relaxed and her fingers curled once again, but this time to grip my shirt to hold on. I angled her head as I wanted, boldly touching her tongue with mine, licking along her teeth, nipping at her lower lip. She was a novice, untried. A kissing virgin and that had my blood pumping, my cock pulsing against her belly.

No man had touched her before. I knew this from hearing the small sounds of surprise and longing that escaped her throat. I found the corner of her mouth, kissed her there, her cheek, her ear. "No. You're not my kitten right now," I whispered, my lips feather light on the delicate swirl of her ear. "You're my little wildcat."

She would fight me in everything, feel as if I'd corralled her like a wild filly, of that I had no doubt, but it would be quite the journey, this discovery of how it should be. But none of this was a concern for tonight. Tonight I would make her mine, show her the pleasure that could be found in being my wife. I'd show her the passion that was within her and give her a way to let it out, for there was no better outlet for her intense, wild nature than fucking.

"I don't know why I even thought to make you mine in a bed. I'm taking you, Rose, right here, right now. You want to be free, kitten. I'll set you free." My voice was gruff, my breathing deep, my need too great to wait a moment longer.

I stepped back just a sufficient amount so I could undo her blouse, but the buttons were too small for my large fingers. Ridiculous little buttons! I took hold of the two sides and tugged, the material parting easily.

"Chance," she moaned. "Oh, yes."

Buttons went flying into the darkness. I stripped the blouse off her readily enough, letting it fall to the grass at our feet, loving the sound of her breathy consent.

"What the hell is this?" I asked, running my fingers over the white fabric wrapped about her torso. It was bright in the moonlight and it appeared as if she were a mummy from clavicle to navel.

Rose's head lowered, ran a palm over the material. "I...I don't wear a corset."

"*That* is plain to see." I tugged at the snug material but could not find a way to remove it. "What I don't understand is its purpose."

"It keeps my...my bosom minimized."

My fingers paused at her words. For a small woman I always assumed she was petite everywhere—that her breasts were small and pert. I had dreams about her breasts and how they'd feel in my palms. What she was sharing though was a surprise and I couldn't wait to unwrap her, quite literally in fact, like a Christmas present.

"How the hell do you take it off?"

Her hands went to her left hip, where I could discern a small knot. I fumbled briefly, but it came undone and the length of soft cotton fell and circled around behind her. Intrigued and fascinated, I picked up the tail end and pulled, which required Rose to spin around. It was like undoing a frayed end of a knitted sweater, pulling and pulling until it was just a pile of yarn. In this case, Rose circled around like a top, slowly, for I was enjoying the idea of unwrapping my wife until the last of the long strip was in my hand and she was bare from the waist up. Instead of turning to face me, she gave me her back, with her arms up to cover herself.

Her skin was so pale in the moonlight, a gleaming white, and her fair hair seemed dark in comparison. I could see the shadow of the long line of her spine. She would not turn and I smiled inwardly at the modest action of such an unbridled woman. A moment ago she'd been shouting at me, furious, and now she was quiet and demure. Stepping up to her, I placed my hands on her shoulders, which caused her to stiffen briefly, and slid her long hair so it rested over one shoulder. I couldn't help but kiss the elegant line of her neck. The scent of her skin was intoxicating, sweet and floral. It was a fragrance I would never forget.

I felt the frantic beating of her pulse beneath my lips and I kissed along that vertical path that ran up to her jaw and down to the juncture with her shoulder. Beneath my fingertips, her skin was silky soft, and I felt gooseflesh rise as I worked down her upper arms and over her crossed forearms. It was a warm night and I knew it was my touch that brought them about, not a chill. Holding each wrist gently, I lowered her hands to her sides as my lips kissed along her right shoulder. From my vantage point, I could see the full, plump swells of her breasts and nipples so dark in contrast. Her quick breaths had them moving and I couldn't help the groan that escaped.

I had to touch them, weigh them, *feel* them, for they were so unlike my fantasy. They were more.

"Why do you hide these, kitten?" I murmured gently. "They are perfection."

Wrapping my arms about her, I cupped her breasts in my hands—they weren't small at all but a perfect handful—and her head fell back against my chest.

"Because...oh, Chance, that's...um—" She licked her lips.

"Why?" I asked again, pleased to see she was so

responsive. I ran my thumbs lightly over the plump tips and reveled in how they tightened into perfect little tips.

"Because they make me too curvaceous."

That was most certainly true. For her petite frame, they were quite bountiful.

"And because it was too uncomfortable to ride otherwise," she added.

The long strip of fabric was a practicality. Instead of lifting and enhancing a woman's curves like a corset did, Rose's solution allowed her to complete tasks on the ranch that would have been inhibited by plush endowments. A lush figure would also draw unwanted male attention. For that alone, I was thankful for her inventiveness. It had hid her assets remarkably well until I, her husband, discovered them.

"I think you will enjoy having them unbound." And so would I.

Taking each nipple between my thumb and forefinger, I tugged and listened to her moan. It was a combination of a cry and an exhale, yet it made my cock grow thicker and my hips shift into her lower back. I couldn't deny myself—both of us—any longer. Grabbing her hips, I spun her about and lowered to my knees so I had the perfect view of those secret curves.

They glowed in the moonlight, perfect teardrop shapes, her nipples tight and furled. I only had to move my head a few inches to take one into my mouth, the tip firm against my tongue. Her small hands tangled in my hair, pulling me in, holding me in place. I sucked and laved one perfect nipple with my mouth, tasting her sweet illicit flesh, my palm cupping the other as my fingers working the nipple. I heard her moans, felt her fast breathing against my mouth, and could feel her frantic heartbeat beneath my palm.

"Chance, oh!"

I let my hands roam, up and down her sleek back, around her waist, but her skirt was an impediment. I fiddled with the closure, then let the fabric drop and pool at her feet as I switched to suckle at her other breast.

Sitting back on my heels, I took in the sight of her, from her boot covered feet, her stockings and those pretty ribbons that held them up, a small bit of creamy thigh that was exposed below her white drawers, the small indent of her navel, her full breasts, dainty collarbones, slim neck, plump lips, and then...eyes that were wild with the blurry haze of her first arousal.

"You're so beautiful, kitten."

She shook her head, a long tendril slipping over her shoulder to brush over her nipple. I felt jealously toward a wayward curl. One of her arms came up to cover her breasts.

I shook my head. "Oh, no. You're mine now. Every beautiful inch. There's no hiding yourself from me. I'll know all your secrets." I took the hand she used to cover herself and placed it on my shoulder so she could balance as I took off her boots. "There's just one more secret, kitten." I then tugged at the small ribbon at her waist, letting the loose fabric drop to the ground.

I felt her fingernails dig into my shoulder through my shirt. Her pussy—fuck—she was perfection. It was dark, too dark to discern her pretty pink folds, but I could see the hair that guarded it was the same pale color as on her head.

My release tingled at the base of my spine and I knew if I pulled my cock from my pants it would all be over. I'd waited so long for this moment, yet she was a virgin and needed to be ready. "Fearful" or "nervous" or "modest" were not adjectives I'd use to describe a woman who was ready to be claimed for the first time. It was my job to get her ready. And so I did what I'd longed to do; I lowered my head to taste her.

"Chance! What are you doing?" Instead of her fingers gripping me, she pushed at my shoulders, stunned by my very forward gesture. I'd only touched her with my nose before I was shoved back onto my heels.

"I'm going to eat your pretty pussy. Hang on." Wrapping one arm behind her knee, I lifted her leg and placed it over my shoulder so she was wide open for me. She might fight me in this, but I would ultimately win. Although, it wasn't a competition. As soon as she discovered how good I could make her feel, she'd want more. With the tip of one finger, I ran over her slit with the lightest of touches, forward and back, finding her slick and hot, before parting her plump lower lips and finding her clit. There!

I lowered my head again, this time I flattened my tongue and laved her in the path my finger took, ending with a small flick over her hard nub. Now when she called out my name it was for a completely different reason. Her hips bucked and I wrapped an arm about her hip, my palm gripping her lush ass and holding her securely in place. I smiled against her, pleased with her response.

Her taste was mouthwatering. Sweet, yet unlike anything I'd ever tasted. It was perfectly Rose, and I was addicted. Her flesh was hot and wet and scalding against my tongue and the way she responded, the way she tensed and tugged at my hair as I flicked her bundle of nerves had me eager to find out her responses when I was buried deep within her. First, she would come. I would watch her as she found her first pleasure and would drink down every drop of her essence.

With my free hand, I found her untried opening and slowly slid a finger in. Instantly, her inner walls clamped down, holding it in place. She was tight, so fucking tight and that was just my finger. She would surely strangle my cock. Once I got balls deep in her I could easily embarrass myself and come like I was a randy teenager, but I had to remember this was all for her. Her first time needed to be nothing but feeling, nothing but sweet bliss, and I would give it to her. It was my right. It was my privilege, and her pleasure.

I moved my finger, mimicking the motion of what my cock would do in short order. In and out I moved, slipping in a little further each time, quickly discovering her maidenhead, that amazing barrier that saved her sweet pussy just for me. I wouldn't break it with my finger, but with my cock and so I retreated, switching to circling and teasing her instead.

"Chance, oh my. What are you doing to me?"

I didn't answer, only continued, for I knew she was close. With the quick flicks of my tongue and the motions of my finger, it wasn't long before her nails dug into my scalp, her thigh muscles clenching as she came. I looked up her perfect body and saw her head thrown back as she screamed, the quiet of the soft, warm night broken by her cries of pleasure. It was incredible to see, delectable to feel against my shoulder, my cheek, my hands and delicious to taste. Her juices were plentiful as her body became fully ready for my cock.

5

HANCE

As her orgasm abated, her muscles went lax and I lowered her gently to the ground, quickly spreading out her long skirt beneath her. Her eyes were closed, her mouth open as she breathed hard, and the sheen of perspiration across her breasts and belly was bright in the moonlight. One of her legs was bent at the knee, her thighs parted in a way she would have found immodest if she weren't so sated. I took advantage of the moment and undid the placket of my pants, my cock springing free and pointing toward the woman it would fill.

I didn't hesitate, but lowered myself, placing my hands on either side of her head. Using my knees, I nudged her thighs wide, settling my hips in the cradle of hers. My cock bumped against her hot, wet flesh and I groaned.

"Kitten, look at me." My voice was deep and rough as it came out through gritted teeth.

Her eyes fluttered open and she looked up at me, so innocently, so sweetly, so aroused. I couldn't resist lowering my head and kissing her. Instead of being tentative, her tongue eagerly met mine and the kiss turned carnal. Her motions were innocent and she had much to learn, but her eagerness had a will of its own. My hips shifted of their own accord, nudging my cock over her slick folds, and then nestling at her opening.

I lifted my head, met her stormy gaze. "You're mine, Rose, just as I'm yours."

I couldn't wait. I ached with every muscle in my body to not only fill her, but claim her. After this, there was no going back. She'd be mine completely. Pushing forward, the wide head of my cock stretched her open. She was so tight, so hot, and I hissed as I sank slowly into her. Only the sound of our breathing and distant crickets filled the air. The moonlight made her surprised eyes sparkle, her skin glow. Her nipples were tightly furled and her hair a thick curtain behind her head. As I bumped into the barrier of her virginity, I knew then that I was home. This was where I wanted to be. The Goodman ranch could burn to the ground. Locusts could swarm and eat all the grass. The cows could all die from a blizzard. None of that mattered as long as I was with Rose. I wanted to fill her up as she'd done to me.

"Mine," I whispered, lowering my head to kiss her when I carefully broke through that last barrier to making her Mrs. Chance Goodman. I swallowed her cry of pain with my lips, soothed her with flicks of my tongue. Lowering to my forearms, I stroked a hand over her face, wiping a stray tear that had slipped down her cheek.

I was fully embedded inside her, the head of my cock nudging at the opening to her womb. Her inner walls clenched tightly, as if her body were afraid I'd leave. Rose's hands pushed, then pulled at my shoulders as her hips tried to shift beneath my heavy weight. I wouldn't relent, wouldn't ease up at all, for the only way for her to accustom herself was if I remained within.

It wasn't easy. Hell, a tooth pull from the town doctor was less painful than my cock deep within her and not being able to move. She needed time to let the pain recede, for once I started to move, there would be no stopping. She wouldn't want me to.

"No more pain," I murmured. "Only pleasure, kitten. Only pleasure."

She nodded her head in short little motions, although she probably doubted me. When, and only when, she relaxed beneath me, her fingers unclenching on my shoulders, her thighs relaxing against my hips, did I pull back, slowly and very easily as she was dripping wet. Then I slid fully into her once again.

Her eyes widened, her lips parted. "Oh," she whispered.

I grinned. "Like that?"

This time when she nodded her head there was less worry and more eagerness. So I did it again. She shifted her hips and arched her back and I slid in a little bit further, and this time we both groaned.

"Holy hell, kitten, you feel so good."

"Yes, Chance. I...I had no idea." She licked her lips and that had me lowering my head, licking over the same spot myself. I kissed her as I began to move in earnest. She was so small in comparison to my large frame and I tried to take her gently, but when she lifted her hips and began to meet me thrust for thrust, I couldn't hold back. This was supposed to be a tender, sweet first time, but she would have nothing of it. Of course, she wouldn't. This was Rose. *My* Rose. She did everything with zeal, with her entire being and that included fucking. And so I didn't hold back. I plunged into her and her head fell back. I grabbed hold of her hip and angled her just right and began to fuck her. Hard.

"You want it hard, Rose?"

"Yes!" she cried. "More."

Sweat dripped down my temple as my breath soughed from my lungs. I relaxed my grip on her ass—she'd surely have marks there—and grabbed the inside of her knee, pushing her leg back so she was spread wide. This allowed me to take her harder, faster and deeper.

"It's...it's going to happen again. No, don't slow down. Please, Chance. I need—"

She didn't say anything more because I ground my hips into hers, my body rubbing against her clit as she came. This time, instead of screaming, she cried out my name, then lost her voice altogether. I took a moment to watch her as she came, but I couldn't focus for long. My baser need took over, my balls drew up and my seed shot forth. I came with my own shout, filling her with pulse after pulse of my seed, marking her. I'd made her my wife in name earlier. Now she was mine in body as well.

ROSE

Chance lay replete on top of me, the brunt of his weight on his forearm, his head nestled at my neck, his warm breath mixing with mine. He still filled me, although I could feel wetness seeping from my...pussy, but I had no energy to move, to question anything. The stars overhead were bright and scattered like dust across the sky, twinkling down at me from the vastness. It made me seem so small; the Montana prairie could do that as well. In this moment, it was also Chance who made me feel small. He was so large, so virile. So potent.

I had no idea it would be *anything* like that. I'd imagined it to be...pleasant, but this had been like the fireworks I'd seen at Fourth of July celebrations. I'd felt as if I had touched the stars in the sky. It was Chance who'd made me feel that way.

I absently ran my hand up and down his back. "You're wearing all your clothes," I commented. I could feel his pants against my thighs, his shirt against not only my palm, but also my bare breasts and my belly.

"You're wearing your stockings," he countered. Lifting his head, he looked down at me. It was too dark to see much, but I could see his smile, see a glint in his eye. "Do you want me to take my clothes off?"

It was a dangerous question for a maiden, although I was one no longer. If I said no, then I would not get a chance to feel his warm skin, to see what the hair upon his chest looked like and see if it matched my imaginings. I'd seen a glimpse of it at the opening of his shirt a time or two, but nothing more. I'd seen the dusting of dark colored hair on his muscled forearms, but never higher. I wondered if his legs would have similar hair. And then there was his manhood. I felt it big and swollen within me, but what did it look like? If I said yes to his question, would he consider me a loose woman? I bit my lip, unsure of what to say.

"Do you, kitten?"

I rolled my eyes at the ridiculous endearment. Who called someone kitten? I was forgetting his question. He watched me carefully, earnestly even. This was Chance and I couldn't lie to him. He knew my secrets, now more than ever. "Yes," I whispered.

When a grin split his face, I knew I'd answered correctly and relief—as well as heat—swept through me when he sat back on his haunches. Only then did his cock slip from me and a trickle of wetness seeped out in his wake. My legs were positioned on either side of his and I was spread wide open. Naked. Exposed. I tried to pull a leg back, but he shook his head.

"You can't be shy now." He worked his shirt off and I forgot all about that shyness as I watched inch after inch of his body revealed. It was dark, quite dark to get a full glimpse of him, but the moon was bright and it was ample enough. Only when he'd tossed the shirt to the ground beside me did I notice his manhood.

"Oh my," I muttered.

He looked down his body, then at me. "Ever see a cock

before?" He held up a hand. "Wait. Don't answer that. The only answer you can give is no."

It was my turn to smile at his possessiveness. "No. I've never seen one before." I looked at it, mesmerized, and even gasped as I saw it pulse, then lengthen before my eyes.

"See what you do to me?" he asked.

"Is it...is it always like that?" I came up on my elbow so I could get a better look. I couldn't discern color in the darkness, but the thatch of hair at its base was of similar color to what was on his head, his forearms and the smattering on his chest. His cock was thick and long and I could see a shadow of a vein running along the side of it. At the top, it was broad and wide. Overall, it was quite imposing. That had fit in me?

"Around you? Yes."

"I...I never knew."

"Good," he countered and I saw a pleased expression on his face. He seemed quite happy that he'd been the one to deflower me. "Knew what, exactly?"

I was thankful for the darkness because I blushed. Silly really, considering what we'd just done, where he'd had his mouth, but I did nonetheless. "I can't say."

He quirked a brow as he sat on his shirt, undid his boots, and then shucked off his pants. I watched him the entire time and hadn't even thought to close my legs and he moved to kneel between them once again. He placed one hand on the ground by my head, blocking my view of the stars. "What, kitten? No secrets."

"It's a little embarrassing. Quite a bit actually."

"I promise I won't laugh." His gaze dropped to my

breasts and he began to gently stroke a finger over my shoulder, my collarbone and then lower, curving over the swell of my breast. I arched my back into his touch. I had no idea it would feel so good, or that he'd find my breasts so fascinating. Then he pulled his hand away.

"Chance," I replied, pouting. I liked his hand there exploring me.

"Tell me."

He was going to withhold his touch until I told.

"I thought...when a couple...um, did it—"

"Fucked?" he added.

"Well, yes."

"Say it, kitten."

"When a couple fucked."

"Good girl."

I took a deep breath, let it out. "I thought that when a couple fucked that the man was like a bull."

6

OSE

I CLOSED my eyes and threw my arm over them. There, I couldn't see him now.

His finger returned to its gentle caress at my breast. It seemed if Chance got what he wanted, I'd get what I wanted in return. I felt my skin heat at just the slightest touch of his fingertip.

He remained silent, only his fingertip moving, then retreating altogether.

Before I knew what happened, he had me about the waist and flipped over. I put my hands out to keep from falling on my face and Chance pulled back on my knees so I was on all fours. He moved in close behind me so I felt the hairs on his chest tickle my back as he loomed over me. He was warm, his skin radiating heat like a cast iron stove in January.

"You mean like this?" he asked, his voice husky.

I didn't know what he meant until I felt his...cock nudging at my entrance once again. He must have been holding it, guiding it over me because he used it very precisely, like a decadent weapon. It slid over my heated, slick skin, bumped that spot that he had licked a short while ago and had made me feel unbelievably blissful.

Then I felt his finger—it was too small to be his cock —slide into me. I clenched it tightly with my inner muscles, the feelings it elicited making me groan.

"I love feeling my seed in you, knowing I've marked you as mine."

"Chance, you are quite possessive," I told him, my voice a rough rasp.

I felt him kiss his way up my spine as he slowly fucked me with his finger. He was remarkably gentle and surprisingly tender. I loved it. When he reached my neck with his mouth, he whispered to me.

"You want me to be the bull, kitten?" He pulled his finger free and I felt it replaced with the broad head of his cock at my opening, then nudging inside. I was too slick to resist—not that I wanted to—and he filled me in one smooth stroke.

"Oh!" I cried. There was no pain this time, only incredible pleasure. It was different this way; he was able to go deeper, filling me so full that I felt as if we were one. Then he pulled back, almost all the way out and I could feel my lips there spread and cling to him.

"I'm going to fuck you now." His voice was filled with intent and it most definitely was not a question. He wasn't asking me if I felt amenable to being fucked again. He was just going to do it.

"Yes," I replied, liking the way he was taking charge. I had no idea what I was doing. He did and I was thankful for it. I wanted him to show me everything that we could do together. And for once, I didn't have to think. I could just *feel.*

And then he moved. This wasn't gentle. He'd been gentle before, but not now. I realized he'd held himself back, but no longer. He pulled back and rammed in, his hips striking my bottom hard, the sound of flesh on flesh filling the air. This wasn't romantic. This wasn't sweet. It was carnal. It was rutting. It was animalistic. And I loved it.

"Yes!" I cried.

My breasts swayed beneath me with every deep penetration. Chance's large hands gripped my hips and he took me, filling me over and over. I was still aroused from the last time I found my pleasure, and my entire body was awakened and sensitive to everything that Chance was doing. Inside, his cock slid over places that sparked to life—that sent heat and brightness through my body. My nipples tightened, my body was damp with sweat even in the soft breeze. My hands gripped the soft grass beyond the material of my skirt as if anchoring me to the ground, for on one perfect, deep stroke, he set me on fire once again. I cried out, letting him do what he wanted for it felt...so...good. He wasn't just taking, he was giving. Giving me the most sublime pleasure I'd ever felt.

I was aware of being shifted, but I didn't care, the pleasure continued. I felt one of Chance's arms band about my waist, holding me to him. He'd pulled me up so I sat upon his thighs as if he were a chair, my back to his front. I could do nothing from this position except let him lift and lower me. I could feel his cock fill me, pressing deep as his other hand cupped my breast and plucked at a nipple.

"One more time, kitten," he breathed. "Come one more time and I'll go with you."

He pinched the tender tip and then tugged on it. I hissed out a breath as it stung, but it morphed into heat, as if a blanket warmed my body, and the delicious pain mixed with his cock so unbelievably deep had my entire body tightening, tensing and this time, there were no words.

Chance's breath was hot at my neck, his groan of completion a surrender of sorts, and I felt his cock thicken within me as he coated me again with his seed, hot and thick. My head fell back against his shoulder. I felt well and truly claimed and there wasn't anything I wanted to do about it. If this was what being Mrs. Chance Goodman was like, it wasn't so bad after all.

I AWOKE TO SUNLIGHT, a soft bed, a strange room and a naked man beneath me. I remembered Chance helping me dress after he'd...fucked me, not once but twice. He didn't put me back into all my clothes, however, for he'd tucked my drawers and wrap into his saddlebag. Later, I vaguely remember being carried, but that was all. Now I was warm and surprisingly comfortable as I lay across

Chance, using him as my pillow. My head fit snugly beneath his chin and I straddled one of his thighs. My breasts were pressed into his solid chest and I felt his breathing, that even rise and fall, beneath my palm.

I'd never before slept with a man, let alone *on* one.

In just a short time, perhaps twelve hours or so based on the angle of the sun through the window, my life had changed entirely. I was now Mrs. Chance Goodman. I'd left Rose Lenox out on the prairie when he'd taken my virginity.

"Are you sore?" Chance's voice was gruff with sleep. He hadn't moved at all, but he'd somehow known I was awake. A hand settled on my back and began a leisurely slide up and down.

It was a good thing he couldn't see my face for I could feel my cheeks heat. "I am not accustomed to speaking of such things," I replied like a persnickety spinster.

"What? Your pussy? Fucking? I should hope not."

"Why do you call it that?" I asked.

He lifted his knee so that I rode his thigh, my pussy grazing over his hard muscle. I moaned at the contact. I'd never felt such as this when I rode a horse or touched that part of my body. Why did I respond so with Chance?

"It's your pussy because it makes you purr when I stroke it. And that's why I call you kitten. Not only are you a little wildcat, but I knew you'd be a passionate lover."

I turned my face into his chest, but he wouldn't allow it.

"Look at me, Rose."

He waited patiently for me to turn my head so my chin rested on his chest. His eyes were dark, his cheek rough with the start of a beard. He needed to shave, but I didn't want him to. I'd never seen him this unkempt and I felt a wild sense of satisfaction knowing I'd made him this way. That I was the only one to see him like this.

"There's no shame in showing me your body, telling me what feels good and then letting me give it to you. You belong to me. Your body belongs to me." He nudged his thigh a little higher. "This delectable pussy belongs to me."

He rolled us so I was on my back and he loomed over me, lowering one hand between my legs to gently stroke over me, watching me carefully. "Now, answer my question. Are you sore?"

I wasn't sore, but I felt well used, as if instead of riding a horse, I'd been the one who'd been ridden. Perhaps, I had.

"No," I replied, my body awakening beneath his light touch.

"It was too dark to see you last night."

He shifted again, lowering his body so he was settled between my thighs, his big hands spreading them wide.

"Chance!" I tried to push him away because of a quick flare of modesty, but there was no give. He was too big, too strong for me to do anything but succumb. I knew the man well. He was always adept at his tasks and never left anything incomplete. If he was going to look at me, I knew he'd give me my pleasure while doing so.

I had to glance down my body at him as he looked his fill, one of his fingers lazily stroking over every part of me. He slipped over my hair there, then over my outer lips, then my inner folds to find that spot.

"Oh, there," I sighed. I might have been modest, but when he touched me, I wasn't afraid to tell him what I liked. And I liked *that* very much.

He glanced up at me. "Right there? That's your clit. Your hair on your pussy is so pretty, but it's in my way. Later, when you have your bath, I'll shave you."

I frowned. "Shave me?"

He ran his finger through my pale curls. "I want you nice and slick and smooth when I eat your pussy again. Don't worry. I'll leave a pretty little patch of hair right here." He tapped the spot just above my folds.

"Now where was I?" His finger moved lower. "Here?"

He made me forget all about being shaved in a most intimate place when he touched where his mouth had been the night before. "Oh yes. I...I like it when you touch me there."

"Good girl." He grinned. "What about here?" His fingers spread my inner lips and his fingertip slipped inside me, but only a little bit. "There's a spot inside that I think you're going to like. I'm going to find it very soon and when I do you're going to—"

I groaned and my eyes slipped shut as his finger ran over this amazing place.

"Right there?" He nudged it again and again.

"Yes," I hissed.

"Rose." When my eyes met his, he continued. "I'll make you come, but for now, we're going to discover what makes you burn."

"I think...I think you've found it," I said, my breath coming out in little pants.

The pleasure was building, akin to the night before. I

recognized it now, savored it, *wanted* it, but he was not going to give it to me. Yet. His finger slipped free.

"Chance!" I cried.

He slowly shook his head from side to side, smiling wickedly, that dimple all of a sudden terribly annoying. His finger continued on a path of discovery, but this time, instead of going the way I expected, it dipped lower and over that dark place.

"Chance!" I tried to clench my legs together but between his broad shoulders and other hand, I could not escape.

"Oh, you've never been touched here. Never knew about ass play, did you? If you really don't like it, then I'll stop."

His fingertip gently brushed over that illicit spot and then began to circle, pressing in slightly. It felt...odd and yet, incredible. After having him awaken my clit and then finding that spot inside of me, what he was doing with his finger merged it all together, as if forming some sort of ball of pleasure and I couldn't control it. *He* controlled it.

"Should I stop?" he asked.

I bit my lip and shook my head, let out a breathy, "No." It was completely wrong, but with Chance, I didn't mind... all that much.

"I'm going to fuck you here too, kitten. Someday soon when I've prepared you."

OSE

THE MENTAL PICTURE he painted was dark and tawdry and very, very appealing.

"There's something wrong with me," I said, wriggling my hips.

He paused in his ministrations, but did not move his finger. "Are you unwell?" A little frown marred his brow.

"I shouldn't like this."

That dang dimple reappeared along with his brilliant smile. He lowered his head then and got to work, as if playing with my pussy and my...ass was his reason for being. "So I shouldn't stop?"

I shook my head again.

"Good. As for liking it? Oh, yes you should. I love that you're so wild, that you like when I play. Put your head back, kitten. Close your eyes. Let me take care of you. I love to take care of you."

"But—"

"Shh," he soothed. "You have all the say, remember?"

He would stop if I told him to. I knew that about him. He was pushing me past anything I'd ever imagined, but that didn't mean it didn't feel good. We were in the privacy of his bedroom. Alone. Safe. I could share with him my darkest secrets, secrets I hadn't even known I'd had.

"Don't you want to come?" he asked.

Yes. Yes, I did. I bit my lip, then nodded.

"Good girl." Using his other hand, he circled a finger around the opening to my pussy. The combination was remarkably intense. "Then do as I say, close your eyes and I'll make you scream."

Realizing I couldn't fight him or what he was doing to me any longer, I let my head fall back on the pillow and let my eyes slip closed. It was true; I could do nothing but savor his attentions. I didn't want to do anything else. I panted when he started pushing his finger into my back entrance, but it didn't hurt. His other finger provided ample distraction. I had no idea how long he played, but when his fingertip breached that tight ring of muscle, he used his other hand to work that spot inside my pussy and I groaned, a mixture of surprise and pleasure.

Chance was no novice, but an expert at working my body. I came instantaneously, my muscles clenching down on both of his fingers as the hot, scalding pleasure washed over me. I did just as he said. I screamed.

AFTER A SIMPLE BREAKFAST, we rode home. Well, to the Lenox ranch which was home up until the day before. I'd grudgingly agreed with Chance that I share the news of our wedding with my family. It wasn't the news that had me dragging my feet while I'd dressed, but the fact that I would be returning as a failure. It hadn't even been a day, and here I was, riding up to the kitchen door rather than a ranch of my own. I'd failed at my dream.

Chance dismounted his horse first before helping me down as everyone came spilling out from the kitchen to meet us. As I went up the porch steps, Chance tied off the leads to the rail. I glanced at all of the familiar faces and I offered a weak smile.

Miss Trudy stood with hands clasped together, quiet and calm as ever. Miss Esther had a frown on her face and her hands on her hips as if she'd known I'd cause them all grief. Dahlia, Marigold and Iris watched and whispered to each other.

Chance's warm hand on my elbow surprised me. He'd removed his hat.

"Something you want to tell us?" Miss Esther asked, looking down at my attire. I had on the skirt I'd worn the day before, but Chance had ripped the buttons clean off my blouse in his haste to bare my body, so I wore one of his shirts, the bottom tails tied together about my waist. It was so big that I had to roll the sleeves up.

What she couldn't tell was that I wore no drawers. Chance had told me they'd been lost out on the prairie. Those words I doubted to be true, but that didn't make them appear. So I was naked beneath my skirt. Not only that, but Chance had helped me take a bath a short while earlier, and then actually shaved me as he'd promised. He's spread me out on the bed once again, my knees bent and heels spread wide as he set about the task with a very high level of diligence. It had been slightly embarrassing, but the look in his eyes as he'd done it made me feel feminine, wanted and surprisingly powerful. It helped that Chance had done the shaving while he was naked. It allowed me the chance to see the effect I had on him as well, his cock long and hard, a vein pulsing along the length. He had no modesty and when he was done, he hadn't hesitated to fill me up. He'd said he was insatiable, that seeing my pussy all bare with just a hint of curls at the top of my mound had him needing me again. Yes, I'd felt powerful.

I blushed just thinking about it and most assuredly both women, Miss Trudy and Miss Esther, could read my mind, or at least have an idea of my thoughts.

Of the two sisters, Miss Esther was the one who vented her spleen with regularity. She shared her opinion on everything from the saltiness of the soup to the way the owner of the mercantile overcharged for flour. She knew who was courting whom, and could tell a woman if she were pregnant before that woman knew herself. She was the practical sister while Miss Trudy was the calm one. Growing up, they balanced each other well when dealing with eight little girls, like equal weights on a scale. And when she told you to do something, you upped and did it.

I glanced at Chance. Why did he look different today

than just yesterday? He still had the unruly hair, the same clear eyes, that ruthless dimple, that wry mouth. I flushed as I considered the answer. He'd done things with that mouth that would make Miss Esther faint dead away, yet he stood beside me, silent and resolute. I wasn't alone.

"We married," I said, my chin lifted.

Dahlia, Marigold and Iris squealed and shouted, running inside most likely to spread the news to the others, while Miss Esther pursed her lips. "Took you long enough, young man." She wiped her hands on her apron with a nod of her head and went inside.

Miss Trudy was left alone on the porch, although chatter escaped through the open door.

"I see you found her," Miss Trudy said to Chance.

He gave her a nod. "Yes, ma'am."

"You sent him to find me?" I asked her.

"I didn't have to."

I looked between the two of them. "I don't understand."

"I knew from our conversation yesterday you were going to do something rash," Chance replied. "Besides, I had to make sure you were safe before I headed off to Parsons to pick up those head of cattle."

I felt riled at the use of the word "rash." My activities of the night before *had* been rash, but they were *my* rash actions, no one else's. Besides, I'd say the wedding itself had been somewhat rash.

"I'll go visit with Big Ed for a spell." Chance gave my arm a quick squeeze as he leaned down and gently kissed my brow, then turned and headed in the direction of the stable. Fled would also have been a more apt word. No man wanted to step foot in a house filled with ten women, especially the morning after marrying one of them surreptitiously.

"Coward," I called out.

He turned and grinned. "Self preservation," he called. He gave me a little salute with his fingers and turned back around.

"Come inside and have some coffee."

I climbed the steps to the porch and Miss Trudy wrapped her arm about my waist as we entered the kitchen together. Once inside, I took a deep breath in fortification.

"You're married?"

"Chance Goodman is so handsome!"

"How could you not tell us, Rose?"

"I bet you wore those infernal pants to your own wedding."

"What did he do, return you?"

All of my sisters spoke at once and there was no chance to get a word in. They continued their eager questions until they realized I hadn't answered any of them.

"Yes, I married him." I pulled out a chair and sat down, my sisters following suit and sitting down in their usual places around the kitchen table. I'd expected comments about my departure or the reason for leaving, not about being married. These questions were remarkably easier to tolerate.

"Is it like they say?" Poppy asked, her voice hushed.

"Yes, does Chance make you happy...*in the bedroom?*" Dahlia added.

I could feel my cheeks heat and when I glanced at Miss Trudy, she didn't offer me any aid, only gave a woman's smile. She stood by the stove and poured a cup of coffee, just following the conversation from the edges. I had joined the married women's club and I now knew why the maidens remained without a clue. I had absolutely no interest in sharing any details about what Chance and I had done or what he told me he planned to do soon. How could I?

I'd not known the things we'd done were even possible, and still couldn't be sure that other couples did them. Did other husbands take their wives from behind just like rutting animals? Should I have liked it so much? Did other husbands shave their wives...down there? Did other husbands put their mouths on them? My entire body warmed at the thought. I knew if I couldn't think about it without blushing, I most certainly couldn't talk about it. Besides, most of the things we did hadn't been done in the bedroom.

"Chance is...is—"

Seven eager faces stared at me, reminding me of when we were little and Miss Trudy read us stories.

"What?" Dahlia asked. "Handsome? Smart? Funny? Nice?"

"Well, yes, but you knew all that. He's lived nearby forever."

"So why did he marry you? Hyacinth's older," Lily remarked.

Hyacinth lowered her gaze and a bright red flush crept up her cheeks. "I am not interested in Mr. Goodman, Lily, and he knows it. I think Rose is his perfect match."

Bless Hyacinth, for she was always the calm voice of reason. I hoped she found a man of her own, for she was deserving of his love.

"I'm not so sure about that, for the wedding was a surprise," I said.

"You didn't know?" Marigold asked, eyes wide. "How romantic!"

"Tell us how he found you," Miss Esther asked. She was folding clothes from a basket placed at the end of the table.

"I was in Clayton and he talked me into it." I was not going to mention my predicament with the other man or the events on the second floor of the saloon.

"That's it?" Daisy wondered. "Did he ask you?"

"Did I ask her what?" Chance came through the door and all heads turned to him.

"Did you ask Rose to marry you?" Daisy repeated.

Chance glanced at me. "Of course, I did. Miss Trudy, Big Ed wanted me to tell you the wheel on the wagon's fixed and that he received a letter from his son and he'll be joining him soon. The letter was fairly long in coming, so he could arrive anytime."

"Jackson, yes. I've hired him to help out around here."

"You weren't going to tell me about him?" I felt as if she'd punched me in the stomach, the very idea she'd planned to give my job to someone else painful.

She gave a soft shake of her head. "It was only a matter of time, Rose, before you left. Besides, Big Ed isn't getting any younger. I'm sure having his son with him will make the man happy."

"Maybe he's handsome," Dahlia cooed, shifting from the claimed Chance to the possibilities this stranger possessed.

I could only roll my eyes at her singular focus.

"I doubt you've had a chance to gather your things," Chance added, placing his hands on my shoulders.

I shook my head and looked up at him. I was glad he'd come inside, for the questions would have gone on forever. I stood.

"Just collect some clothes, for now. You can get your other things another time." He leaned down and whispered directly into my ear so only I could hear. "Pack a corset, kitten, or you'll go bare." His breath fanned over my ear and I shivered.

"You seem to be in a rush. Are you going somewhere?" Lily asked, completely unaware of what just passed between us. I had an inkling why he seemed to be in a rush. Lily, on the other hand, did not.

Chance looked at Lily and grinned. "Do all newlyweds get all these questions or is it just from you, brat?"

Lily grinned and flushed, pleased with the attention Chance was giving her. "Just from me."

"You're my sister now, so you keep the boys away. Or else." Lily was the youngest, although only a few months younger than me. She was also quite lovely and I had no doubt suitors would be flocking to her like bees to honey soon enough. Chance had good reason to be protective.

"You didn't answer her question," Dahlia said.

Chance came around the table and wrapped his arm around my waist. "I know," he told Dahlia.

8

OSE

"ARE WE REALLY GOING SOMEWHERE?" I asked, once I'd packed a bag with some of my clothes. I'd hugged and kissed everyone and promised to visit after our return—from wherever it was he'd planned. Our horses plodded along side by side, the morning still cool, yet the sun warm. We both wore hats to shield our faces and necks from the intense rays.

"I've put the cattle drive on hold for two days," he replied. "Until then, we're not leaving the house and if I have my way, we won't be leaving our bed."

My mouth fell open. "What? Then why did you infer otherwise?"

"So they'd leave us alone. If they knew we were home, we'd have visitors stopping by all day long. You have seven sisters, kitten, and they'd plan the day so that each one came by at a different time. They're crafty like that. Except Hyacinth."

What he said was true. My sisters, being conniving busybodies, would invade like a plague of locusts, and bother us all day long. Hyacinth wouldn't stop by until she received a written letter of invitation or I dragged her to the house by her hair.

"You know my family well. If we're not going anywhere, then what are we going to do?"

He grinned. "It's been three whole hours since I've had you last. I've been a neglectful husband."

I flushed at his words and was surprisingly eager for him to remedy his neglectfulness. We weren't back yet though. "What's this about a cattle drive? I heard you mention it earlier."

We went over a rise and Chance's house—my house —came into view. The vastness of his property could be seen from this vantage.

"I see you've changed the subject. Until we get to the house, I'll answer your questions. Once inside, the only words I want to hear from your pretty lips are *Please, Chance* and *more*. Deal?"

I couldn't help but blush and wonder what he'd do to make me utter such things. I felt my nipples tighten in anticipation. "Deal."

He sighed and shifted in his saddle. "It's a contract that I signed over the winter. I told you about this, at least in passing, and it's time for the cattle to be moved."

"How many head did you buy?"

"Five hundred."

I couldn't help being surprised by the quantity of

cattle he was taking on. His ranch was successful—I'd always known this—but since he'd taken over after his parents died, it had thrived and grown three- or four-fold.

"When do we leave?"

"For Parsons? The men and I leave on Wednesday."

I nodded. "Good, I'll be ready."

He turned his head and looked at me. "Oh, no. You're not going."

I gave the reins a slight tug and stopped my horse. "What do you mean I'm not going? I thought I was going to run the ranch with you. This is part of it."

"Going on a cattle drive with a group of randy and unmarried men is no place for my wife."

"If I was a man you'd let me go," I countered.

"If you were a man I wouldn't have married you."

"So you're just going to leave me here to embroider?" I waved my hand at the large ranch, outbuildings and animals dotting the landscape.

"Hell, no. Your embroidery is terrible. I'm leaving Chappy and Walt behind, but you can't be alone with them. They're good men, but it seems I'm a little protective."

I'd heard their names before but never met any of Chance's ranch hands. He had quite a few with a spread of his size. I was coming to realize he'd kept me away from them on purpose.

"Then what are you going to do with me?"

"Send you back to Miss Trudy."

My mouth fell open and I felt my cheeks heat, and it wasn't from embarrassment this time. "You...you're sending me back to live with the girls? What are they to think? That I've failed you? Just like I failed in leaving Clayton, is that it? You're giving me back?" I narrowed my eyes. "I see. You've fucked me and now you're going to send me home."

Chance was a peaceful man. A calm man. I'd never seen him overly riled until now. The night before in the saloon when he'd faced my perpetrator he'd been riled, but this? I'd never seen Chance like this before. There was a little tick in his jaw and his eyes narrowed. When he spoke, his voice was very, very quiet.

"You better get that horse moving, kitten, before I catch you. If you aren't in that house when I do, I'll lift that skirt and spank your ass wherever you are."

Spank my—

My eyes widened at his very quiet, very lethal sounding voice. I'd pushed him too far, but he'd done the same with me. When I saw him reach toward my reins, I nudged my horse with my heels, spurring him into action. The animal seemed pleased to be allowed his head and took off as if he were being chased. Perhaps we were, but I wasn't going to look back and find out. If Chance wanted to spank me, he'd most certainly have to catch me.

CHANCE

ROSE WAS UNCONTROLLABLE. If she thought, even for an instant, that I would take her along on a cattle drive, then she must not have known me at all. I may have let her go off on wild hairs when she was younger, but she'd been safe on the Lenox land, where little more than her pride could be hurt. But childish imaginings and dangerous antics of a grown woman were two different things entirely. The previous night, she could have been raped. Going on a cattle drive was akin to spending the evening playing cards in a saloon. The men were rough, the language crude and their sexual bents talked about over beef jerky and thick black coffee. It was no place for a lady. Hell, it was no place for a woman, lady or not.

It was no place for my wife.

I wasn't leaving her behind because I didn't want her. Hell, if she could have seen how hard my cock was, she'd have known leaving her was the last of my desires. Why would I want to leave a voluptuous and voracious lover for a miserable week in the saddle? I'd rather sink into her plush pussy in a comfortable bed than sleep alone on the hard ground with a saddle for a pillow.

Unfortunately, Rose didn't have the same perspective and that only got her into trouble, as she spewed unreasonableness that had my palm itching. And so she'd fled. Good. It gave me time to cool my head, for I would never deal with her antics while angry. I was going to spank her perfect ass until it had a pretty pink glow to it and she was limp and contrite across my lap. And then...then....

I spurred my horse to catch up and only did so when I was inside. I found her standing behind the comfortable chair by the fire. I spent many a long winter night reading in it as the weather raged outside. Now, however, her anger raged inside.

"You are not going to spank me," she vowed.

I hung my hat on the peg by the door. "I am," I countered. "You're getting five for your complete disregard for your safety last night and you'll get five more for your ridiculous ramblings."

Her eyes widened and her hands gripped the cushion of the chair. "Ridiculous ramblings? You're going to give me back!"

I slowly walked toward her and she retreated, one step back for every step forward. Her legs were much shorter than mine and I quickly gained ground. "Why the hell would I want to give you back?"

"Because you're done with me," she replied. Her gaze darted over her shoulder to look for any impediments in her path. There was only one. The wall.

I pointed to the front of my pants. "Look, kitten. See that? That's right, my cock. It's so hard it could pound nails in a fence post and do you know why?" I took one more step and she bumped into the wall. She couldn't move in either direction with a desk on one side of her and another wall on the other. "Because I want to fuck you all day long. I'm always like this when I'm around you. It's been like this for months. *Months*, Rose. You shouldn't be afraid I'll give you back. Instead, you should be afraid that I'll never let you go."

Her mouth fell open and her eyes widened. I'd finally stunned her quiet.

"Now you are going to turn and bend over the desk

and lift your skirt for me and I'm going to give you the spanking you've been itching for."

"I do not want a—"

I held up a hand. "Not another word." I waited as she considered her options, which were none. Then I watched her swallow as she thought about what was to come. I doubted she'd ever been spanked before, for if she had she wouldn't be behaving so recklessly.

She turned and placed her hands on the dark wood, then leaned forward. Her compliance had my cock press painfully against my pants. She knew I wouldn't hurt her. She knew while I was riled, I'd never spank her when truly angry. She didn't know it, but she was lost. A firm hand was needed because she couldn't see that I'd be there for her. I'd protect her, cherish her, love her with all my heart. She'd been loved at the Lenox house, without doubt. But she hadn't had one person focus solely on her. She was scared and lashing out. I'd be there for her, even if it meant a spanking to settle her.

And that was the crux of the problem. She didn't know that a spanking from me would actually settle her and until she did, she'd fight me like a wild mustang.

"Lift your skirt, kitten. Show me what's mine."

She tossed a dirty look over her shoulder, but remained silent, her hands reaching down to lift up the length of her skirt, exposing her trim legs one inch at a time. Finally, the little ribbons on her stockings appeared, then the creamy pale skin of her thighs just before the lower curves of her ass, then finally the full globes. She placed her hands before her once again, her face turned away. She might not see it, but deep down, this was exactly what she wanted.

I lowered down to my haunches and removed her boots and stockings, then leaned in and kissed on pale globe before standing again.

When I placed my palm on one lush cheek, she startled and I soothed her. "Easy, kitten. I've got you. You've been trying to get my attention since you were eight years old with your antics. I saw you then and I see you now. The difference now is that your wild deeds will get you spanked. You've got me, kitten, all of me. You don't have to make me angry to have me take control. I'll fuck you—don't you worry none about that—but I'll decide when."

I brought my palm down onto her upturned ass. She jumped at the crack that filled the air, but the strike wasn't overly hard.

"Hey!" she cried, but could do nothing with my hand at her lower back.

Spank.

"You have me, kitten, by the balls."

Spank.

"Seeing you like this, with your pretty ass turning nice and pink."

Spank.

I nudged her feet apart. "Your pussy's pretty and open. I bet if I run my finger over your smooth flesh I'll find you slippery and wet."

Spank.

"You want this. You *need* this. You need me to take control."

9

CHANCE

WITH THAT, I finished out the ten I'd promised her, then plunged my fingers into her sopping wet pussy, easily filling her with not one finger, but two. She pushed off the table with her hands, arching her back.

"Chance!"

"You like that, don't you, kitten? The way I rule your body? You're going to come for me." I placed my thumb over her distended clit and pressed firmly as I worked her with my fingers. "Right now."

She did. She came on command, milking my fingers as if she never wanted to let them go. Her juices dripped onto my hand as she screamed, her entire body taut. I continued to work her expertly until the last bit of pleasure ebbed and she slumped back onto my desk. I would never be able to look at the wooden surface again without seeing her this way.

As I stepped back and lifted my wet fingers to my mouth, tasting how sweet and wild she was, she pushed up and turned around to stand before me, her skirt falling back in place. She lifted her gaze to meet mine.

"You think you control me?" she asked, her voice smooth as silk after her orgasm.

"I know it."

Her hands went to the knot at the bottom of my shirt that she wore, undid it. Then she began working free all the buttons down the front, one at a time. She didn't shift her gaze away from mine. "You think you have all the power, that I'll just bend over a desk and let you have your way with me."

I grinned, and I watched as she dropped the shirt to the floor. "You just did," I replied cockily.

She undid the knot on the wrap that circled her torso, worked it around her body with ease and proficiency, her ripe breasts coming unbound.

I stifled a groan at the sight. With the sunlight streaming through the windows, she looked almost golden, her hair wheat colored, her skin a pretty flushed pink. Her nipples were plump and I ached to suckle at one as I remembered their taste. Sweet and tart just like she was.

Next, she undid the fastening and her skirt fell to the floor.

"You have the power?" she asked again, this time stepping up to me and pressing her palm against my pants directly over my hard length. The tips of her nipples bumped against my chest.

I hissed out a breath, shook my head. "Power? Absolutely not. That's all you, kitten. Remember, you can always tell me no when I take control."

She pushed me back so I bumped into the wall, letting her have her way. She was correct, I may be the one who was in control, but she had power, like a sorcerer's spell bewitching me. I'd followed her to town to keep her safe. I'd spanked her ass because she needed a keeper and needed to know her boundaries, but even so, she held all the power. And now, with my cock beneath her palm, I'd let her do whatever she wanted.

When she dropped to her knees before me, undoing the placket of my pants and grabbing my cock in her tiny grip, I was stunned. I was even more so when she put the wide head into her mouth and licked over the little ridge along the bottom as if she were voracious.

"Jesus, kitten," I groaned, my fingers tangling in her silky hair. "Where the hell did you learn this?"

She didn't answer and the way my eyes rolled back in my head, I didn't need to hear it. I just felt. It was incredible, hot and wet. She took me in deeper while still gripping the base. Then she started to move, in and out. She wasn't overly skilled, her motions more eagerness than adeptness, but hell, if she kept it up for much longer, I'd come. I felt my orgasm tighten my balls, felt the seed boiling and ready to burst forth. I gently pushed her off me and my cock throbbed at the loss. It was wet and shiny from her mouth, the color an angry red.

When I started to back her up so I could lay her once again on the table and fuck her, she shook her head. "No. I'm in control now."

And how I didn't come then and there from those sultry words, the look on her face, her naked body, I had no idea. She was so passionate, so wild when she released all of her inhibitions. I took a step back and towed off my boots, then stripped off my clothes in all haste. I leaned against the wall and slid down, bending my knees slightly with my feet planted on the floor. "All right, kitten. Ride me. You control it all."

She looked down at me, saw my erect cock, clear fluid seeping from the tip. It took her just the briefest of moments to understand before lowering herself down to her knees so that my cock nudged her scalding hot pussy. Straddling me, she placed one hand on my shoulder for balance then grabbed hold of my cock with the other. I hissed out a breath as she guided me to her opening and lowered herself down. Our eyes met and held. She was so wet that I filled her quickly and we both gasped, almost startled by the ease and swiftness of penetration.

"There you go, kitten. I'm all yours." Her inner walls clamped down on me like a vice and I gritted my teeth at the sweet feel of her.

Her eyes fell closed and her mouth opened, her breasts rising and falling with her little breaths. She was the most amazing sight. I couldn't resist touching her and so I lifted my hands and cupped her breasts, heavy and plump, running my thumbs back and forth over her nipples and watched them harden.

"Chance!" she cried, then started to move, lifting her hips up and down, but she wasn't taking all of me and couldn't settle.

"Lean back," I told her.

She shifted slightly, her back against my thighs and I slipped in all the way. "Oh," she sighed.

"There you go. Now you're crammed full. I've given you control, kitten, so make me come."

It wasn't an outright dare, but she took it as such, beginning to move with earnest. I released her breasts and watched them sway and bounce as she shifted up and down, then rolled her hips in circles to rub her clit over me. Her innocent, untried motions were my undoing, having me come as I would if she were the most skilled whore. I gripped her hips and held her in place as I filled her completely, my seed jetting forth in hot pulses, filling her.

We were both breathing hard, our skin coated with perspiration. Her forehead rested against mine, and when I opened my eyes, her green ones were right there, all blurry and passion filled. Her skin was flushed and she was feverish with need. I couldn't help but kiss her, our mouths meeting in a wild kiss. It wasn't soothing her, only adding to her eagerness to come. She pulled back and I ran my finger over her wet, swollen lower lip.

"Good girl. Your turn now."

"Oh yes," she whispered, beginning to move.

My cock hadn't softened at all, still a thick rod within her, but as she began to ride me, fucking herself, my seed seeped out, the sound of her motions filling the room.

The scent of our joining was thick and redolent and yet I spurred her on with words.

"So beautiful. I love feeling your pussy squeeze my dick. Feel that? Your pussy's overflowing with my seed. Your nipples are so tight, kitten, they must ache."

I felt her inner walls grip me just before she bowed her back, thrusting her breasts up to my mouth. She screamed her pleasure, and I couldn't help but take one tight tip into my mouth, tasting the saltiness of her skin. Her fingernails dug into my shoulders and I would have marks there for some time. I didn't mind, hell I loved knowing she'd marked me, just as I'd marked her with my seed.

Slowly, slowly, her senses returned. A small smile formed on her lips. Her eyes were dreamy and her skin was dewy and glowing. The sight of her after her pleasure was perfection.

"Again," I said, moving my hand between us to rub my thumb over her distended clit. She was dripping wet and I was easily able to work her to orgasm. She was so sensitive and just as easy to bring to pleasure after the first time.

"Chance, I...oh!" She closed her eyes, yet only shifted her hips slightly, the release a soft, sweet one in comparison to the first.

"That's my girl," I whispered, pulling her into my arms so she rested against my chest. "Now, tell me, why the hell would I want to give you back?" This was home—Rose in my arms and my cock filling her. There was no place else I wanted to be.

"I CAN'T BELIEVE you're making me do this," Rose said, as we rode up to the Lenox house. The closer we came, the surlier her demeanor grew.

She'd grudgingly packed a bag with some clothes for the stay with her family while I was gone. It would be about a week, but if I had my way, I'd push through to make it shorter. When I'd signed the contract over the winter to gain the head of cattle, I'd had no idea I'd have a bride to leave behind.

"I just spent two days fucking you, kitten. I figured you'd recognize who's in charge by now."

She turned in her saddle. "Are you saying that one time you let me be in control was just pretend?"

I tipped my hat back a tad so I could see her better. "Did my cock pretend to be hard? Was all that seed that filled you pretend?"

"That's not what I mean and you know it," she countered, her voice prim.

"You can take control any time you wish when we're fucking because it's hot as hell."

She shook her head with what I assumed was disgust. "You're such a bastard." Clucking her tongue, she spurred her horse to quicken her pace. I did as well to keep up.

I tsked her. "Language, kitten. You didn't enjoy yourself?" I loved to talk dirty to her, loved to see the flush that came over her cheeks, the prim way her posture straightened and her attitude changed to that of a virgin schoolmarm. I'd fucked her good and hard for two days straight. She most certainly was not a virgin, but she was still quite innocent, and it was endearing.

"You know I did, but still."

I sighed. There was nothing I could do except explain it again. We'd had this argument over and over the past two days and each time there was no resolution. I only fucked her until she gave over to me, to the pleasure. It seemed the only time she gave herself completely was when I filled her with my cock. It was the only time I heard the words "Yes, Chance," uttered without complaint.

"Rose, you can't go on the cattle drive because it's dangerous and the men are rough, at best."

"You're going," she countered.

"I'd rather not go altogether, but this is how we're going to build the herd. I can't do my work and worry about you at the same time." The thought of her dealing with crude men or even a stampede had my blood chilling.

"Why would you worry?"

"Because you're my wife!"

"I thought we were to run the ranch together," she continued.

I took my hat off my head, ran my hand through my hair, put it back. "Did it ever occur to you that you might be with child? I might be protecting you, but you need to protect a baby."

Her mouth fell open but no words escaped. "A baby? You can't be serious."

"Dead serious, kitten. How many times have we fucked? How much seed did I put in your belly? I bet some's dripping out of your right now. There's no question we made a baby, and if not, it won't take long the way we can't keep our hands off each other."

"But—"

"No buts. You're staying put until I return."

10

OSE

MY HUSBAND RETURNED ME. Even though it was only temporary, it felt like I'd been used and left behind to live once again in a house full of women who seemed hell bent on driving me to insanity. I'd run away to Clayton because of it and after ten minutes I was ready to do so again. The only difference this time was that I was legally bound to Chance.

I was no longer Rose Lenox, but Rose Goodman.

"You must have been a terrible wife to be delivered home after only three days." Poppy's words stung.

Lily and Iris laughed along with Poppy at her joke. They were the last in the kitchen finishing their breakfasts. The other girls had gone off to do their chores or to read, sew or other vacuous task.

"If he wasn't pleased with you, do you think I could be his wife next?" Lily giggled.

I pursed my lips and dug into my eggs, ignoring them. My chest ached with the deep need to be free of this house, and not because I missed Chance, either. No, I didn't miss the man at all, or his very skilled hands. His mouth. His cock. I squirmed in my chair. I missed him *too* much.

"Maybe he'll find someone else on his trip that satisfies him more," Dahlia said, coming into the kitchen to pick up a pair of scissors.

I'd ignored the barbs so far as it was just poking fun, but there could be a hint of truth to what Dahlia said. Could he meet another woman while he was gone? Would he find her more biddable and less contrary?

The eggs lodged in my throat and I had to take a gulp of hot coffee to wash it down. I placed my fork on my plate, food forgotten.

Miss Esther clapped her hands and shouted over the din of the girls' laughter. "All right, all right, let the poor girl breathe. Lily, go out and tell Big Ed to hitch up the wagon. We're going into town for supplies. Dahlia, wrangle your sisters. Poppy and Iris, hold your tongues."

I sat at the table, content to watch the family as they hurried about their business. Bonnets were donned, reticules claimed and the group was out the door. How eight women could leave the house within a minute was remarkable; Miss Esther no doubt had them prepared, which meant my return had been foreseen. I hadn't told them; Chance had kept me too occupied to even think of them. Only Miss Trudy and I remained.

The lingering scent of coffee and bacon filled the air. The room was warmer than outside, the stove emitting an ample amount of heat, although the back door remained open to allow it to escape.

"You knew I'd be back," I said.

"Chance sent Walt over yesterday. He wants you safe, Rose."

Miss Trudy took a seat across from me.

I frowned. "He wants to keep me from running the ranch."

"Has he said something to that effect?"

"He wouldn't let me go on the cattle drive!" I dropped my fist onto the table making the dishes clatter.

"Has he prevented you from helping in other areas?"

I could feel my cheeks heat. "Well...." I squirmed. "I haven't exactly had the chance."

"You do look happily wed," she countered, looking me over.

"Um...thank you?"

"He doesn't please you?" For the first time, Miss Trudy sounded concerned.

"You're more worried about his being a good lover than his control over me?"

"Well, is he?" Why did she have to be so dang calm?

"An accomplished lover? Yes!" I replied, shouting.

"Then what is the problem, young lady?"

"I want to run my own ranch," I countered.

"Yes, I'm aware of that. So are your sisters, Miss Esther, Big Ed, as well as your husband."

"Everyone knows?" I thought I'd kept my dreams secret, but that did not appear to be the case.

"There are no secrets here. You know that."

I looked down at the worn table. It had seen so much of our lives. Meals, school work, everything was done while sitting at this table. Now, my first conversation as a married woman was here as well.

"I can't have my dream if I'm married, especially when he keeps me from participating."

Miss Trudy stood, went over to the coffee pot. I hadn't even noticed she'd put it on to boil earlier. "Why ever not?"

"Because *I'm married!*"

Miss Trudy turned to face me. "I think you're going to have to explain yourself, for I do not understand."

"You did as you wished, and you weren't married," I replied.

She didn't answer right away. Instead, she turned and retrieved her cup and filled it. She blew on the hot liquid and took a sip before speaking.

"When I was sixteen, my parents were too poor to feed me. I'll skip a few details, but I found myself on the doorstep of a brothel, where I worked as a whore for the next ten years. Esther, as my younger sister, appeared on the brothel's doorstep a year after me and we slowly saved our money and bought the business from the woman who ran it. We went from homeless to whores to madames. Neither of us could marry, for we were too tarnished. Husbands weren't for either of us; too many men had crossed our paths. What neither of us had, but both desperately wanted, was a child."

She took a sip of coffee, letting her words settle. I

knew a little of her story, but this was the first time she'd shared it all.

"Then came the fire. Such devastation. Somehow, through that tragedy, God gifted us with you girls. Imagine, eight orphans! And girls, oh, we knew all about girls. We wanted all of you. There was no decision to be made. Esther and I just sold the business, took our money and eight tiny girls and started over. Here in Clayton."

"You took just what you wanted from life, without a husband," I said.

She took her seat, and smoothed down her dress. "Do you think I wanted to become a whore? That I wanted to watch my own sister follow me into the profession? That my childhood dream was to work on my back?"

I felt contrite at her words. "No, but—"

"Do you think I wanted to run a brothel? I wanted other things, but sometimes life doesn't work out as you plan, Rose. Looking back, though, God gave me just what I wanted."

She meant us girls. She'd wanted a child and received eight!

"I don't want children right now," I replied.

"Based on the very satisfied look on Chance's face earlier, you may want to think again about that."

I just glared at her, wishing she and Chance didn't have such similar thoughts. Why did they have such insane notions about what kind of wife I should be—that I would be birthing a baby before the winter? There was no way we'd made a baby. I'd know if I were expecting and I felt the same, albeit sore in very new places and definitely loose muscled. I should be *with* my husband, not left behind like a weak-willed woman. I should be on the cattle drive with him. Beside him. As Miss Trudy left me to complete her daily tasks, I formulated my plan.

CHANCE

THE TRIP WAS FUCKING MISERABLE. An hour out of Clayton, it started to rain—a veritable deluge that made the creek swell, forcing us to backtrack to a spot where it was easier to pass. One of the men fell off his horse and broke his leg. I had to let another man accompany him back to Clayton for the doctor, as it was closer than Parsons. By that point, there were just two of us forging on in the wet. It didn't let up the first night. We had to sleep under a stand of Ponderosa pines that did little to shield us from the elements. The rain didn't stop until we were an hour outside of Parsons and by then, neither of us cared where the hell we were as long as there was a bed. But there wasn't. The only boarding house in town had burned down the week before so we had to bunk in the livery with our horses.

I missed Rose and our bed. Hell, I missed Rose. A bed wasn't needed. We'd proved that readily enough in the past few days. Besides my desk, the stairs, the front door, the kitchen table and even the hip tub were exceedingly pleasurable places to fuck one's wife. I shifted uncomfortably in my seat in the home office of Jim

Reeves, the man who sold me his cattle. A cock stand was not something I needed while closing out our business.

"It's good to have you here," the other man said, smiling amiably. "Although I'm sorry to hear about your man breaking his leg. And to top it off, the one who made it all the way to Parsons is sick." He shook his head.

Powell, my man who'd ridden into Parsons with me, fell ill after his night in the livery, most likely from being cold and wet, and was settled in the Reeves' bunk house recuperating.

"Yes," I replied.

"I'll send two of my men with you in his stead. It's all I can offer this time of year, but a herd like that isn't something one person can manage alone."

I nodded, relieved. "I'm much obliged."

Mr. Reeves was older, perhaps middle fifties, with salt and pepper hair, a portly physique and a mild demeanor. His equally mild daughter came into the room then, carrying a tray with two mugs of coffee and slices of cake. I stood at her entry.

"May I introduce you to my daughter, Beatrice?"

She was quite pretty, with dark hair and eyes. Her build was slim and willowy and her smile warm.

"Hello," she said.

I nodded and held my hat in my hands.

"Ever since my wife passed on, Beatrice has been such a help here." He came around the desk to get his mug from the tray. "I've been telling her about you."

I inwardly groaned, knowing the direction of this man's thoughts. It usually came from women of the same generation, who were usually referred to as meddling mothers or even matchmakers. Having a father eyeing a match for his daughter was new to me, but with no mother, it was kind of him to assist in finding a suitable husband.

"Oh?" I asked neutrally.

"When we met in the winter, you seemed a fine young man. I thought, being as you're here on the ranch and all, that you might want to take a day and visit."

I arched a brow, unsure of what to say. Money had exchanged hands, but moving five hundred head of cattle wasn't an easy task. I had men to muster, food to gather in preparation for the trek to my ranch, and no time to linger and socialize. But, I couldn't insult the man in his own home by declining his invitation. I could, however, resolve this situation quickly enough.

"That's mighty kind of you, Jim, and you as well, Beatrice, but I'm newly married and I have a hankering to get back to my bride as quick as I might."

Beatrice flushed to the roots of her dark hair.

"I had not heard the news. Congratulations are in order," Jim said, shaking my hand.

"While I may not be an eligible suitor, I will most certainly share with your father some names of men who I feel would be worthy of a woman such as you." She was quite fetching, and if I judged her based on her father's demeanor and kindness, she would make quite a catch.

She nodded and excused herself. I couldn't blame her hasty departure, but there was no way to make the blow of embarrassment any less. "I'm sorry if I've hurt her feelings."

Jim sighed. "No, don't be. She isn't the one pining for a husband. I'm the one who wants her to be happy."

He moved back to his chair behind the desk, so I sat again as well.

"Is it her dream to be married?" I asked. I was surprised by my own question, for it was the thought of Rose that prompted me to ask.

"Dream? She's an accomplished painter and would love nothing more than to travel around the area painting landscapes. Summer or winter she'd be with her brushes."

I looked up at a lovely painting on the wall. A winding river cut through a verdant prairie, thunderclouds building in the distance to make it striking. "Is this one of hers?"

Paternal pride showed on his face. "Indeed."

"She's excellent. Would having a husband help her with her dream or stifle her?"

Jim frowned and I held up my hand.

"I ask because I'm newly wed and I wonder if I've trampled on my wife's dreams by binding her to me."

Jim nodded in understanding. "It's all about sacrifice. Both people in the marriage will have to sacrifice. I'm guessing your wife will sacrifice quite a bit to meet your vision of marriage."

"She believes she is," I countered.

"Now, I'm just an old coot, so you can ignore my words if you wish, but my sweet wife Laura put up with not only me, the ranch, the cattle, Montana winters and everything that went along with it for thirty-two years."

He took a sip of his coffee. Nothing he'd said so far

sounded any different than what Rose wanted.

"She also had to put up with birthing and raising five children."

My mug was halfway to my mouth and I paused. Five?

"Four boys and then Beatrice. My eldest son lives in his own home on the property, and the three other boys live on spreads of their own. They're all married, except for Beatrice. Seven grandchildren."

"Congratulations," I replied. "Quite a legacy."

He nodded. "To be sure. Laura wouldn't have traded the children for the world, but she gave up a part of herself in raising them. Me, I ran the ranch. Still do. But children grow, make lives of their own. I think Laura would have wanted to make her own mark on the world, instead of helping all of us make ours."

I drank my coffee as I thought about what he said.

"A woman's going to sacrifice more than a man will ever know for her children. If you're blessed with them, her sacrifice will be heftier than yours. Meet her halfway, young man, in all things."

"That's sage advice, sir. May I ask you one question?"

He nodded.

"If your wife wanted to join you on a cattle drive, would you have let her?"

His eyes widened. "Hell, no."

I relaxed in my chair.

"I did let her help sort the animals after and brand them. If your wife wants to get her hands dirty, let her. Then take her off somewhere and get the rest of her dirty."

He winked at me and I couldn't help but grin.

 HANCE

IT WAS the second day out of Parsons and the cattle were fanned out in a wide line moving east at their slow, plodding pace. We followed behind on horseback, the three of us spread out to maintain control. The one on the right flank, Ivers, led a stray back into the herd. Overall, their job was to keep the cows wandering in the right direction. The sun was behind us, the air cooling as the evening began to settle. It had been a dull day, fortunately. Excitement on a cattle drive meant something was wrong. Fortunately, with the rains there wasn't any dust to kick up to choke on. There was nothing but open expanse of prairie in front of us, Cottonwood trees dotting a creek in the distance. It was while I was considering how much the creek levels had receded when I saw her. A rider at such a distance should be unfamiliar, but I knew her well. I knew every line of her body, every creamy patch of skin, every soft sigh, even her scent.

Rose.

Holy hell, the woman had the gall to disregard my every word and wish. The woman was going to be the death of me and we hadn't even been married a week! She rode right through the center of the cattle line and directly toward me. I spurred my horse to meet her.

Her hat was low on her head, her hair pulled back in a single braid that hung thick and long down her back. She wore her usual work attire of blouse and pants and I glanced left and right to see if the men noticed her. Of course, they noticed her! They'd have to be dead to miss seeing a beautiful woman in the middle of a damn cattle drive! She was akin to a mirage in a desert; the men were probably wondering if she were real. She was beautiful, so fucking pretty it made my chest hurt. The sun was on her face, cast her in a soft glow, the long tendrils of hair that had come free of her braid looked like spun gold.

"Is there something wrong at home?" I had to be rational and give her an opportunity to provide a reasonable, logical reason for her defiance. "Is someone sick?"

She looked at me with confusion. "No, of course not. Why?"

"I wanted to see what kind of life threatening problem existed to have you show up against my wishes."

Her chin rose defiantly. "These are my cattle now, too."

"They'll be your cattle when they are grazing on our land as well. What the hell are you doing here, Rose?"

Her chin tipped up defiantly. "If we are going to run the ranch together, then I should be involved. You can't just leave me behind!"

I thought back to Jim's words, how sacrifices had to be made. Her safety was not one of them. Neither was letting the men see her in pants. Her figure, those shapely legs, were for no one else to see. Hell, I was a greedy man when it came to Rose.

I glanced left and gave a shrill whistle. The nearest man, Stills, turned my way and at my hand motion, rode over.

He glanced at Rose, even raked his gaze down her body, lingering in places that made me see red. I cleared my throat and he looked to me, although not in the least bit quick enough for my liking. I ground my teeth together, wanting to put him in his place, even wanting my fist in his nose. But neither the words nor the actions, were fit for Rose to witness.

"Can you two handle the herd for the night?" I said instead.

The man gave a curt nod.

"I need to see to my wife." I didn't give the man more time than to tip his hat to my bride before I grabbed her reins and rode off.

We headed westward back the way we'd come, heading toward a creek and one of those groups of Cottonwoods. With the men and cows headed in the other direction and the large trees sheltering us from view, we had ample privacy. There was no one about. I dismounted, and then dropped the reins to the ground to let the animals walk to the creek to drink. I took off my hat, ran my hand through my hair, and then hooked the hat onto the pommel of my saddle.

"Get down, Rose."

She eyed me carefully, but easily swung her leg over. I put my hands at her hips to help her down whether she needed it or not.

"You're angry," she said, crossing her arms over her chest. Clearly, she wore that wrap to bind her breasts, as I knew now the bounty they were. They were hidden well, and for once, I was thankful for that infernal contraption —glad the men hadn't seen all of her lush curves.

"Angry, kitten? Let's talk about the reasons why I might be upset with you." I held up my hand with a finger raised. "You defied me when I said you couldn't come on the drive."

She humphed, but did not reply.

I raised my second finger. "Did you even let Miss Trudy know where you were going or did you just disappear before the sun came up?"

She looked away and I knew my answer.

Another finger went up. "Did you ever consider that you could be in any kind of danger, alone on the prairie?"

Instead of looking away, she turned around so I had her back.

"What's the first rule you learned growing up?" I asked.

I heard her mumble something but couldn't discern the words.

I put my hands on my hips. "What was that, kitten?"

I took a step closer.

"I said, always tell someone where you're going." She sighed.

"Why is that, pray tell?"

She tilted her head to the side as if she were a recalcitrant adolescent. "Because there are dangers everywhere and no one will be able to find you if you were hurt."

I took the few steps that separated us, took hold of her shoulders and spun her around. I knocked the hat from her head, letting it fall to dangle by the string down her back. "If you'd been bitten by a rattlesnake, I would have been two more days on the trail before I even knew you'd left, then I'd have had to go and search for you, over a vast prairie and by then you would have been dead!" My voice went up as I spoke. I couldn't help it. I gave her a little shake then stepped away.

I was breathing hard and I felt my pulse racing.

"I'm sorry!" she called out.

"Sorry?" I turned my head to look at her. "Jesus, Rose, you could have fallen from your horse or been hurt some other way and I couldn't have helped you."

"You should have taken me with you to begin with," she grumbled.

I pursed my lips and counted to ten. I went down to my horse, which hadn't ventured far eating the tall grass, and grabbed my bedroll. "We are not going to discuss my decision again." I spread the blanket out and pointed to it. "Now, you are going to get on your hands and knees, drop your pants and I'm going to give you a spanking you won't forget."

"I will not!" she shouted. Her eyes were filled with fire, every line of her body defiant.

"Where are you going to go, kitten?" I lifted my arms in the air. "There's no one here. Scream all you want, but you know you deserve a punishment. You put yourself in danger and that is not allowed."

"Chance!"

"It was going to be twenty-five, but now it's thirty."

"Chance." Instead of hearing indignation in her voice, I now heard pleading.

"Forty." I crossed my arms over my chest, not willing to back down in the slightest.

She grumbled something as she pulled the string for her hat over her head. With no grace whatsoever, she got onto her hands and knees, then looked at me over her shoulder.

"The pants, kitten."

When she was going too slowly, I helped her, reaching out and undoing the button, then tugging the snug fabric down over her hips. How Miss Trudy allowed her to wear the pants in the first place was beyond me. The fact that she'd continued to allow her to don them after she became a certain age just showed how relaxed rules had been for Rose. She needed guidance. She needed direction. She needed a firm hand. It was my job to give them to her. Right now.

When the pants were around her knees and her perfect ass was visible, I sucked in a breath. She was a sight to behold, punishment or not, and my cock didn't care either way.

"I'm pleased to see you aren't wearing any drawers."

"I don't have any," she grumbled. "It seems whatever pairs I took with me to your house have disappeared."

I sighed, let out some of my frustration. "*Our* house." I paused, letting that sink in. "You were in a household of all women. How could you not find a pair to sneak for yourself?"

She looked at me with utter shock. "We do *not* share underthings."

My mouth ticked up in a smile. "I'm glad to have discovered one rule you will not break."

She frowned.

I moved to sit on the blanket, Rose settled over my lap, bottom up. She squirmed and wriggled, but I held her in place.

"Why are you being punished?" I asked.

"Because I was reckless with my safety."

Smack.

She shifted forward at my strike, but did not move. I spanked her thrice more, hitting a different place each time. Her ass was turning a lovely shade of pink and a handprint formed on the upper swell of her right cheek.

"Why else, kitten?"

"I disobeyed you."

I gave her five more rapid spanks. As she shifted, her discomfort obvious, her knees parted and her pussy became visible. I could see her perfectly shaved skin and her pretty pink folds. In the waning light, I noticed the glisten of her desire. She liked what I was doing to her, dominating her as I was.

"What else?"

Lowered on her elbows, her hands tightly grasping

the blanket. When she shifted position, her pussy became even more open, her petals spreading and I saw every perfect inch of her. I stifled a groan, as I wanted to lick her pussy and make her come. That would have to wait, for we weren't done with her punishment.

"I...I don't know!"

Spank.

"You are not to wear those pants in front of the men. It shows off your woman's shape. Your body is for me to see, no one else."

Spank.

My palm tingled as I finished out her punishment, watching her flesh darken from a pale pink to crimson. I didn't spank her overly hard, for the count was high. My cock was hard against the placket of my pants, uninterested in her spanking but in what was soon to follow.

Once finished, I exhaled and ran my palm over her hot flesh, letting the sting seep in.

"You're wet, kitten. Do you need something else from me?"

Her eyes were closed and she rubbed her cheek against my blanket.

"Say it. Tell me what you need."

She looked back at me. "I need you."

"Where?"

"Inside of me. I need to come."

Yes, the way she was wiggling her hips, I knew she was as eager as me.

I didn't stall, but moved her from my lap, but kept her on her forearms and knees. I didn't even remove the remainder of her clothes, for I needed to be buried in her, knowing she was mine and that she was safe. My fingers deftly undid my pants, pushed them down enough to free my cock. Shifting on my knees, I lined up to her sweet opening, grabbed her hip, and filled her to the brim. She was so tight, so hot and slick.

She cried out and I groaned.

"That's it, kitten, just where I want to be. Deep inside you."

12

HANCE

I PAUSED for just a brief moment, and then began to move. This wasn't going to be gentle, nor romantic. This was fucking—down and dirty fucking and we both needed it. I'd been away from her too long and it seemed she felt the same. Not that I wanted her on the damn cattle drive, but we'd take the edge off of our need. Then I'd work out the rest.

She was so wet the sounds of it filled the air. The scent of her arousal was heady. My hips pumped into her at a consistent pace, my cock driving my motions more than my mind. Just the feel of her squeezing my dick had my brain going foggy. I could feel my orgasm building, the scalding heat of her hard to fight. Her hips started pushing back into me, meeting me as I filled her with the slapping sound of flesh on flesh. The sunlight made the skin of her ass a fiery red from her spanking, the remainder of her exposed flesh a bright gold. Her hair was a wild tangle, her braid sticking to the sweaty nape of her neck.

"Do you want to come, kitten?"

She nodded her head. "Yes! Oh, yes please, Chance."

I slowed my pace, reached around and ran my fingers through her wetness, stroking over the swollen nub of her clit. As I continued to fuck her, I began to work her higher, carefully, slowly, yet very deliberately.

"Oh!" she cried out, her body's motions losing their consistent rhythm.

"Not yet. You can't come yet."

"Why?" she cried out, turning her pleading gaze to me. Her green eyes were bright and wild.

"Do you feel out of control? Desperate? Frantic?" My words escaped with my heavy breaths. I didn't stop working her body.

Her eyes widened when my fingers stopped. "Yes," she groaned. Her hips shifted back and my cock pressed incredibly deep.

"Good. Now you feel as I did when I saw you ride up. This marriage won't work if we're both out of control. We'll both go insane." I continued my patient thrusts of my cock, the slight shifting of my fingers, but it was at a cost. Sweat dripped down my temple, my cock desperate to let my baser needs take over and shift to all out fucking. Rose, however, had to know how I felt. "God, Rose, you feel so good. This is where I belong, filling you. Do you know how hot it is to see you like this? To see your pretty pussy lips wrapped around my cock? If something ever happened to you—"

The need for her was too much and I pulled back and thrust deep once again. I couldn't hold back any longer. "Do you understand?" I growled.

"Yes," she replied, her voice needy but almost a little forlorn. Contrite, perhaps? Was I naive to think a fucking alone would make her see reason? Did I always need to have her beneath me for her to understand how much she meant to me? Could I ever let her up?

Moving my hands, I gripped her hips tightly, shifted her, as I wanted to have my cock rub just the way I wanted.

"Reach down and touch yourself. Play with your clit until you come. I want to see you do it." My words were rough as my breath soughed in and out of my lungs.

Lowering herself to a shoulder, she reached down and began to play, the sounds of her breathing changing immediately. I felt her inner walls clench tightly and I knew she was close. It never took much to take her over the edge. The little breathy sounds were an indicator and so I pulled back and made very slight fucking motions just inside her opening, using the broad head to rub over that spot that she loved so much.

It only took three or four passes and she came, her entire body tightening as she called out my name. I couldn't hold back, couldn't resist another moment and I plunged into her, bumping her womb again and again. My balls tightened, my seed boiled and I erupted, the days of abstinence having me coat her insides copiously.

Rose slumped down on the blanket. Her eyes were

closed and her breathing began to slow. Recovery was difficult, as I was still hard and wanted her again. Pulling my cock free, I watched as my seed slipped down her folds. It was such an intensely manly feeling, seeing my wife sated and marked, knowing she was mine, that this seed perhaps would take root.

I sighed and stood, fixing my pants and tucking my shirt in. No matter how much I wanted to stay on the banks of the creek and have my way with Rose again and again, the herd was moving closer to home and we needed to catch up.

I went over to her saddlebag and dug around, surprisingly finding a skirt. I pulled it out and walked back to Rose, who now lay on her side watching me.

"You want to go on the cattle drive? Very well, but you must wear this skirt over your pants. I will think about what is beneath the entire way home, the men will not." I growled the last, for Rose was a beautiful woman and I knew wearing the skirt for additional modesty would not help in this matter.

ROSE

THE CATTLE DRIVE was worse than I could have imagined. I'd envisioned spending the days riding on the beautiful prairie, watching cows plod along until we were on Goodman pastureland. This was a ridiculous fantasy and a complete fallacy. From the moment we returned to join the men, I was miserable. Besides having a sore behind and having to sit a horse, we never rested and the food was dried beef, tinned beans—cold and eaten directly from the can with a spoon—and water. Chance didn't leave my side, giving any other man who even glanced my way a look that would have cut a weaker man dead. And so within the first hour, the men avoided me as if I carried the plague.

When we crossed a creek, swollen from consistent rain, one of the calves lost his footing and was washed downstream. Chance and I followed the line of the creek until it widened where he was able to rescue the wayward animal. Once free of the water, it found a way up the far bank to venture off in search of its mother, lowing pitifully. Our horses weren't so dexterous and as my animal began to climb the bank, it lost its footing and I lost my seat, toppling headlong into the shallow water.

Chance, who'd been beside me, strode up quickly to ensure my wellbeing, but when he discovered my pride was injured more than any other part of me, couldn't help but laugh. I sat in the moving water, soaked from head to toe. My bottom was sore, perhaps from landing upon it, but it could have also been from Chance's spanking and then having to seat a horse directly after.

I stood, the water dripping off me, wanting to grumble, but knew I couldn't. I *could* be comfortably ensconced at the Lenox ranch, instead of soaked to the skin, but I'd made my choice. I'd *wanted* to be here with Chance. I'd wanted to lead our cows to our ranch. Complaining would do me no good.

Fortunately, the water wasn't deep and warm, the sun

hot. I sloshed over to my horse and climbed back into the saddle, which was difficult given my sodden skirt and pants. Kicking my mount into motion, I followed the creek bed further down until there was a more accessible slope. Chance followed, but I could feel his grin and mirth behind my back.

The only pleasure I found the rest of the day was when Chance led us through the inky darkness far from the men, near a different stretch of creek where we washed the sweat, dirt and miles from our skin. I was glad to be stripped of my soggy clothes and Chance provided me with one of his shirts to wear from his saddlebag. Like the one I'd worn a few nights before, it came down almost to my knees and I rolled the sleeves back. This time, however, I did not have a skirt or any undergarments to wear with it. Fortunately, it was soft against my skin and had Chance's distinct smell to it. I reveled in the way his scent wrapped around me. Beneath the moonlight, I watched as he laid out his bedroll once again, and I clenched my bottom remembering what he'd done to me upon it earlier.

"I've never fucked while on a drive before today, kitten. With you here, how can I resist?"

I should have put him off for his brutish display of dominance when he'd spanked me earlier, the intense way he'd taken me and delayed my pleasure, but I couldn't. I wanted him just as badly, and resisting would only prevent me from getting what I wanted as well.

It would be the third time he took me in the outdoors and I reveled in it. There was something different, something almost primitive about being with Chance without a roof over our heads or a bed beneath us. The crickets chirped in the darkness and there was a slight breeze to the warm air.

His hands were working the buttons of my shirt, his knuckles grazing my skin as he did so. As the garment slipped from my body, I felt the freedom I'd craved for so long. I felt uninhibited, naked as I was, outside and exposed—yet only with him. I thrilled at the dark gleam in Chance's eyes, knowing he wanted me so desperately. He stripped quickly, then stepped close so our bodies aligned, his skin hot against mine, our mouths merging in a kiss. This wasn't an angry kiss, but an assault nonetheless. It was akin to possession. His tongue licked over mine, and I couldn't help the moan that escaped. Tugging at the ribbon at the bottom of my braid, he let the locks unravel, let them all fan out over my back.

"I can't get enough, kitten." He leaned his forehead against mine, breathing hard. "I don't think I'll ever get enough."

"Chance, please," I pleaded, wanting his mouth on me again. My lips, my breasts, my pussy, anywhere he wanted.

"Last time was quick. This time, I'm going to go slow."

The idea was so appealing, my inner walls clenched in anticipation. I was just as eager as he was. I felt his cock nudge my belly, looked down at it. I licked my lips, eager to taste him again, to make him lose his mind.

I dropped to my knees on the blanket.

"Kitten," he breathed.

From this position, his very erect cock was within inches of my mouth and my mouth watered. I remembered what he tasted like, how he felt against my tongue. "Tell me...tell me how you like it," I said, looking up at him. I wanted to give him the same pleasure he gave me. I did it freely and with eagerness. I wanted to show him how much I wanted him.

He growled deep in his throat. "Lick it, kitten. Run you tongue over the head."

I flicked my tongue out. He was hard, yet silky soft. There was wetness on the tip and it tasted salty.

"Good girl. That fluid is my cock readying for you. Lick it all up."

I did, running my tongue over the broad head as if it were a candy sucker, the taste of him coating my tongue.

His hand slipped into my hair, tangled there and held me in place. "Just like that. Now take me into your mouth."

I listened to his directions and took him deep, the need to cough made me pull back and my eyes water. "You're...you're too big."

"Grab hold of the base. Yes, like that. Tighter. *Yes*. Now slide your hand up and down the shaft." He hissed out a breath as I did so. "Keep doing that and put my cock back in your mouth. Fuck me with your mouth, kitten."

 OSE

GRIPPING the base as I was, it allowed me to take him into my mouth without choking and I was able to work him as instructed. I felt the thick ridge of a vein up the length and let my tongue slide over it. Once I realized Chance liked what I was doing—the hand in my hair tightened and started to move me on and off him, silently guiding me—I let go of my worries over whether I was doing it correctly and focused solely on pleasing him, on making him come.

I clasped his thigh in one hand to keep my balance. I listened as his breathing changed, felt his cock thicken and lengthen within my mouth, could distinguish his clean scent of arousal on the night air.

"I'm going to come, kitten, and I want you to swallow all my seed. Yes. Good. I'm...coming."

I continued to move my grip as I felt a thick jet of seed coat the back of my throat and I swallowed. Again and again he filled me and I worked to take it all. Finally, his hand relaxed and he exhaled, stepping back so his cock slipped from my lips.

I wiped my mouth with my fingers, feeling a few sticky drops of his seed. Dropping to his knees before me, he stroked my hair back from my face. "You're very good at that, kitten." I could see in the pale light of the moon the way his mouth quirked up. His tone was gruff, relaxed and it made me feel incredible knowing I'd done this to him, made him sated and yet still aroused. Now that I wasn't focusing on him, I noticed that my nipples were tightly furled, my thighs were slick with my own need.

"With that first fuck out of the way—a delectable mouth fuck—it's time to focus on you. We've got all night."

I clenched all of my inner walls at his words. He lowered himself to his hands so he loomed directly above me, dropped his head so he took one nipple into his mouth. The hot feel of that sweet suction had a small moan escape my throat.

"Chance..."

After he laved the tip with tender attention, he breathed on it, the air cooling the wet tip until it tightened painfully. "Like that?"

I nodded.

"Good, if you said otherwise, I'll have to flip you over and spank you for lying."

He moved to my other breast and my fingers moved to his shoulders, pulling him closer.

"It...It scares me that I like it when you spank me."

He stopped at my words, lifted his head. "Scares you? How?"

There was no mocking tone. I only heard the concern in his voice.

"I don't want to like it. What does it make me when I like something as dark as that?"

He kissed me on the mouth, his tongue easily tangling with mine. Sometime later he lifted his head. "It makes you my wife. There's no shame in anything we do together, kitten. Now, let's see if I can get you to be my little wildcat."

DAWN HAD JUST CREPT across the sky when Chance woke me. It was difficult to stir, for he'd been so warm pressed against me, back to front, once he finally let me sleep. I bit back a groan, knowing I could not complain; the trip was my choice. I donned my clothes that had dried during the night, although wrinkled and dirty. The two other men were drinking coffee from tin cups when we rode up. The dark smell filled the air and my mouth watered for some of the eye-opening brew.

"Want some, little lady?" Ivers asked. He was short and stocky and these were the first words I'd heard him speak.

"Yes, thank you," I replied, slipping off my horse's back.

Chance dismounted as well. "We've got another day's full ride ahead."

I reached for the cup Ivers held out. Instead of handing it to me, he dropped it and grabbed my wrist, tugging me harshly into him so the front of my body bumped his. I gasped at the surprising motion.

"Depending on the herd, we could make it to Goodman land by—"

Stills pulled a gun from his hip and aimed it at Chance. I cried out at the sight of the lethal weapon aimed his way. "No!" I shouted.

I struggled against the man's hold, but there was no give. Fear had my mind seizing, unable to make thoughts coalesce. I felt off-kilter, not expecting these men to do something that was rash and dangerous.

"Rose, stop," Chance commanded. I stilled as he bid, but my heart beat frantically.

"Ooh, I like how biddable she is. Now, this is what's going to happen," Stills said. He was tall and whip thin, his eyes narrow and beady. "The lady is going to go off with Ivers while you and I have a little chat."

Chance raised his hands slowly and remained remarkably calm considering. "Let her go. Whatever you have planned does not need to involve an innocent woman."

"Innocent?" Stills grinned as he kept his gaze trained on Chance. "She doesn't seem so innocent to me after the way she screamed last night."

Even with my panic overwhelming me, I felt my cheeks heat. They'd heard what Chance and I had done the night before! It made the acts that Chance said were just between us seem dirty and tawdry.

Ivers chuckled. "Mmm. Perhaps you can show me some of what you did, little lady. I know I'll enjoy it."

Bile rose in the back of my throat at the way his hand moved up and down my arm. If it were Chance's hand upon me, it would be a caress. This man's hand felt obscene.

"Why are you doing this?" Chance growled.

"That's a big herd of cattle. With you dead and us to lead them, they'll be going to our spread."

Dead? They were going to kill Chance and I could only imagine what they were going to do to me. They couldn't keep me alive; I was a witness to their crime. They were going to kill me, but as I looked to Chance for help, I knew what they planned to do beforehand would make me wish I were dead.

Chance's eyes narrowed, his fists clenching.

Ivers dragged me toward a horse. "Up."

I shook my head. "No. I can't."

"Either you get on that horse or I shoot Goodman right now."

I glanced at Chance whose focus was solely on me. "But Chance—"

He nodded and I swung up into the saddle, the gun too big of a risk to argue.

Ivers positioned himself behind me and I held myself erect and as separate from him as possible. We rode north and I looked back the entire time until we went down a small hill and Chance disappeared from view. What had I been thinking? When Chance had said there were hidden dangers on a cattle drive, I'd been flippant, thinking little of his warning. Just as he'd said, I'd grown up trained to tell someone where I was going, even within the borders of the Lenox ranch. Sad stories from townsfolk over the years put value in this effort, but I'd never personally known anyone who'd been saved from harm from heeding it.

I'd always been smart. I knew a rattlesnake hole when I saw one. I knew the clouds that threatened a bad storm. I knew how to put out a campfire to prevent it from spreading into a full-blown blaze. I knew to bring food and water in my saddlebag. I knew not to venture out during a blizzard. I knew it all, or I'd thought I did.

Chance hadn't been stifling me when he left me with Miss Trudy and the girls. He'd been trying to protect me from the things I couldn't control, like the man sitting directly behind me. I'd been bullheaded and silly, flippant even with his concerns. Tears clogged my throat at my predicament, at the way I treated the man I loved. He'd been present for me for as long as I could remember; *I'd loved him* for as long as I could remember. As a child, he'd most certainly humored me in my silly antics designed to gain his attentions. Even now, the silly antics continued and I was still trying to gain his attention, but I'd had it all along. I appeared stupidly at a cattle drive. I wanted him to see me, be with me. Love me. From everything he'd said and done since we rescued me in Clayton, perhaps since I was small, he did love me.

It wasn't ten seconds later that I heard the shot.

"No!" I screamed and fought the man's hold, and then the world went black.

CHANCE

I WATCHED as Rose was taken away, with each step my anger flaring more and more, but the bastard Stills had his gun pointed at me. I could see her directly over the man's shoulder.

"Why the hell do you want to take the cattle? It's a stupid tactic, Stills. It's not as if you can hide five hundred head."

In order to save Rose, I needed to save myself, which meant knowing what the hell was going on. How desperate were these men? Stealing cattle, at least a number of this size, was downright stupid. I had to question their intelligence at attempting such a harebrained scheme. But stupid or not, Stills was the one with the gun and Ivers was the one with my wife. Was this their first theft or was it a routine for them? Was Reeves involved? Did he want the money and the cows as well?

"They're not branded and I plan to sell them, break up the herd."

That was a logical option, a more viable solution than keeping the animals together.

"They'll know I'm missing and come searching," I added. The sun was bright, even early in the morning—it was going to be a hot day—and sweat trickled down my back.

He shook his head slowly, a grin spreading. "I think the coyotes and other animals will find you first."

"And Rose?"

He shrugged. "They'll think she's dead as well, but she's of more use alive to us."

His grin changed from devious to dangerous. There was no fucking way he'd touch one hair on Rose's head. If Ivers did anything to her, he was a dead man. Fuck that, he was dead no matter what.

As I watched Rose and her captor disappear from view, I knew I had to act and act now. A cow moved nearby and lowed, causing Stills to turn his gaze for the briefest of moments. I took the opportunity to throw myself at him, grabbing his gun arm and lifting it into the air. I hit him full out, tackling him to the ground, which made the gun go off, the sound deafening in my ear. It missed me completely, but the animals stirred around us, frightened by the noise.

Anger fueled my motions, and I twisted his wrist until I heard his bones snap. He cried out in pain as the gun fell from his useless hand, but I wasn't done. Sitting upright, I smashed his face with my fist. Blood burst from his nose.

The cows began mooing loudly, their heavy footfall beginning to shake the ground. Looking up, I recognized the early signs of a stampede. There was no way to stop a group of animals if they became frightened. If one did, they all did, following the herd. We were on the ground, right in the middle of the cows. I punched Stills one last time and he slumped down, unconscious. Grabbing the gun from the ground, I rose to my feet, searching for a horse. Any horse. There!

I dashed to it, skirting around wide-eyed, snorting cattle. Climbing onto the equally skittish horse, I tugged on the reins and dug my heels. The cattle began running then, the sound like thunder. It was possible for Stills to have escaped the stampede, but I could only hope for his demise. He was getting just what he deserved for even considering harming Rose. I went with the flow of the animals, following their eastern direction, yet working my way at an angle toward my wife.

The animals could run for a mile without stopping, or fan out across the prairie in all directions. It was the worst consequence on a cattle drive, but I didn't fucking care. Rose was with Ivers and I needed to get to her. He hadn't held a gun when he'd taken her, but that didn't mean he didn't have one. I had to be cautious in my approach; the man's desperation could drive him to do anything.

I slowed my horse, knowing they couldn't have gained too much distance. Now I had to follow and wait, every minute Rose was with that man torturous.

14

HANCE

"YOU CAN'T THINK I'm going to let you watch," Rose said, her voice full of anger.

There had been no place to hide on the prairie with it wide open as it was. A horse and rider would have been too visible and Ivers could have panicked at seeing me and done something to Rose. After about an hour, when I recognized they were heading toward a creek, I had to assume to water the horse, I dismounted mine, left it, and followed surreptitiously up the creek toward them. The Cottonwood trees offered me some shelter, allowing me to slowly get near them, my footsteps muted by the sound of the water. I was thirty feet downstream and Rose was using all the sass. She was the most beautiful sight and the tight band around my chest lessened just seeing her whole and unharmed.

"I can't just let you go off," Ivers countered. "Even to do your business."

Rose put hands on her hips and narrowed her gaze. "Where do you think I'm going to go?" She waved her arms. "You're much faster and stronger than I am. It's not as if I can run away. The water's too shallow to jump in and swim."

Using the man's ego was smart. She was painting herself a defenseless woman, when I knew that to be a falsehood. She was the least defenseless woman I knew.

"I'll stand behind this tree and talk the entire time. Will that suffice?"

"Fine," the man replied, his voice dejected, as if she were wearing him down.

Rose stomped off in the direction of a large tree, but went out of my view. She started talking, loudly, about how she intended to add lace edging to the bodice of one of her dresses, taking the time to describe the color of the thread she'd purchased, then contemplated aloud whether she should add the same lace to the end of the sleeves or whether it would dangle into her soup.

I shook my head and grinned, knowing she was doing this just to annoy the bastard. I doubted Rose knew how to sew, let alone had ever looked at a piece of lace in her life. I'd never seen her wear anything beyond something serviceable and that suited her. She didn't need lace trim to look more appealing to me. In fact, I liked her best when she wasn't wearing anything at all.

"Will you shut your trap?" Ivers called out.

"You're the one who wanted me to keep talking." Rose

came around from behind the tree. "If you don't want me to talk about lace, then I can certainly share with you a delicious recipe for homemade apple cobbler. The secret is adding a touch of molasses to the crumb topping because it bakes up sweet yet melts in your mouth."

"Lady, I don't care if it melts in your mouth or not. Here's what you're going to do, just sit on that rock and just keep quiet."

"Oh, I can't sit on that rock. Do you know what kind of animals live beneath big rocks like that? Snakes! Even prairie dogs and you know they have sharp teeth. I refuse to be bitten by a wild animal while being held captive. When will this captivity end?"

I slipped closer as Rose continued to blather on. If I hadn't known she was doing it intentionally, I would have considered her a vacuous ninny.

"End? You're going to be with us for a while now. We've got plans for you."

"Well, those plans had better be short lived. Oh dear," she said.

"What now?" he grumbled.

"We may have to stay here a bit, for I am beginning to feel a little queasy."

"Queasy?" he repeated.

"Only in the mornings and it comes on suddenly. I would hate to vomit on you while upon the nice horse."

"Vomit? What the hell is wrong with you?"

"I'm expecting, of course. The baby doesn't show very much, what with the full skirt and all, but surely you can tell."

Her words had me freezing in my tracks. Baby? Impossible. Well, probably actually, but she wouldn't know yet. Hell, I would know. She was certainly not far along enough to show as she'd said. What was she getting at now?

"Baby?" Ivers shouted. "Stills didn't say nothing about a baby getting mixed up in all of this."

I moved closer so just a tree separated us.

"It was a surprise to me as well. Do you know how babies are made? because I most certainly didn't before I married. If you're going to keep me around, I shouldn't be jostled and then of course marital relations are not allowed."

"Marital relations? Your man is dead."

"Dead? Good riddance. Clearly you do not have a woman of your own. You know nothing about babies, where they come from or why women marry. There were too many mouths to feed and my father handed me off to that tyrant of a man."

"I heard you screaming your pleasure last night. Hell, the entire territory got wind of it."

"He is—was—a lusty man, but I learned that if I pretended to enjoy it, he'd get done quicker."

Done quicker? *Done quicker?* The woman was going to get a spanking as soon as I got my hands on her.

"Actually, I'm right glad you got rid of him. Now I can travel with you and I won't have a man to worry about. It's not like you're going to touch a woman who's got a baby in her belly."

Ivers grumbled something, then I heard him stomp towards the water. From my hidden spot, I saw him squat down and splash water on his face. Before I could do anything, Rose stooped and picked up a river rock and started chattering again. The man didn't even turn, clearly annoyed with her presence. She lifted the weapon and as he turned to see her approaching, she whacked him on the head. He fell face first into the shallow water with a big splash.

I jumped out from behind the tree. "Rose!"

She turned to me and a look of complete surprise crossed her face. "Chance! Oh my God, I heard the gunshot and thought you were dead!"

I closed the distance between us and Rose flung her arms about my neck, her feet clearing ground. I held her to me securely, then kissed her. She was as eager as I, our lips meeting, our tongues tangling. I held the back of her head in place with one hand, the other around her waist holding her tightly. Knowing she was well and unharmed had all my energy pour into the kiss.

"Did he hurt you, touch you in any way? He didn't—" Fuck, I didn't want her to suffer the horrible impact of having a man use her against her will. If he had, we'd deal with it together, but....

"No," she said vehemently, shaking her head. "He hit me on the head, but I only have a slight headache. Otherwise, he didn't do a thing to me."

I ran my hand over her scalp and felt a lump.

"Are you sure that doesn't hurt?" She could have been addled from a blow to the head, but based on how she'd behaved, her smart actions, I doubted she was injured.

She shook her head.

Relieved, I said, "I think you were making him insane with your incessant chatter."

She grinned. "Good. That was my intention. I remembered the way the girls talk with each other. No man could remain in the same room with the topics they discussed."

"Very smart."

She shook her head, but said nothing.

I looked down at Ivers, and then pulled him from the water so he didn't drown. "Go see if he's got some rope in his saddle bag."

Rose dashed off as I assessed the blow to his head. No blood, but he was out cold. I wanted to hit him again just for hurting Rose, but it wouldn't have been as fulfilling since he was not awake. Rose returned with a short coil and I readily tied him up.

When Ivers moaned, she pulled back, her gaze raking over every inch of me. "I thought he shot you."

I shook my head. "I'm unharmed."

She looked left and right. "Then where is the other man? He could get us, and he has a gun!"

I put a finger over her lips. "Stills won't be bothering us ever again." I left out his gruesome demise as I pulled the gun from the back of my pants.

I angled my head toward Ivers. "We need to secure him better, then go get help."

Rose's hand gripped my arm. "I want to stay with you."

I grinned down at her. "You seemed to have done just fine on your own." She had. She'd used her brain to outsmart Ivers, staying unharmed and waiting for the right moment to save herself. "You didn't even need me."

"Oh, Chance. I'm so sorry! I need you. I need you so much. I should have listened to you and not been so mule headed."

"Mule headed?"

She pursed her lips. "Mule headed and willful. I see now why you didn't want me to come. I will be more prudent in the future."

I eyed her suspiciously.

"Well, I'll try." She looked up at me through her lashes as her hands smoothed over my chest in a placating gesture that I enjoyed immensely.

WE RODE ALL DAY, riding Chance's horse with the lead to Ivers' animal tied off so it followed, to return to the Goodman ranch as the sun slipped low in the sky. I was content to sit within the circle of Chance's arms, sideways across his lap. I could have easily ridden the other horse, but neither of us mentioned it. I would have been too far away and we both needed the physical connection. For me it was to validate that Chance was alive and whole yet I was so weary I nodded off on the journey. It was almost impossible not to; the steady beat of Chance's heart beneath my ear was so reassuring and lulling.

Surprised by our early return, Chappy and Walt came out of the bunkhouse to meet us. After hearing about our complications, they rode off to the Lenox ranch to gain Big Ed's assistance. The older man would ride into Clayton and get the sheriff. At the same time, Chappy and Walt would head west to retrieve Ivers from his bound state by the creek, wait with him, and then give him to the sheriff when he arrived. After that, they'd herd the cows back into a group and on the right path.

I assumed Chance would leave as well, but when he walked me inside instead of saddling a fresh horse, I was surprised. "Aren't you going with them? If you want, I'll go stay with the girls."

"Now you're compliant?" He wiped a hand over his face, making his whiskers bristle; he was probably as weary as me.

"Temporarily," I countered.

The corner of his mouth quirked up. "Then I best take advantage then."

We went first to the washroom, where Chance stripped the dirty clothes from me, one layer at a time. He grumbled when he had to unwind the wrap that covered my breasts, but that was all. I was anxious to scrub the dirt and grime from the trip, but also Ivers' touch from my body. He hadn't done anything inappropriate, but I'd had to sit with him atop his horse and that had been more than enough contact for me.

I took my turn first in the tub, Chance using a cloth lathered with soap to clean me, paying very close attention to specific, very pleasurable spots on my body before washing my hair. I closed my eyes and reveled in the feel of his fingers massaging my scalp.

"Out, before you fall asleep. I need you awake for what I plan to do."

He helped me from the tub and dried me himself, his hands gentle, but every line of his body indicated his eagerness.

"Your turn," I said, working at the buttons on his shirt.

He covered my hands with his own. "If you help, I won't get clean before I fuck you, kitten." The wicked gleam in his eyes showed the truth to his words. "Get on the bed, hands on the headboard, legs spread and wait for me."

15

*R*OSE

"CHANCE...I—"

One dark colored brow arched. "You're compliant, remember?"

I bit my lip and spun on my heel.

I sat down on the edge of the bed and dried the ends of my hair with the bath sheet as I listened to Chance splash in the tub. Using his words as a guide, I had to assume he would not linger on his bath, so I did not linger on my hair. The wild mass was a lost cause; there was no time to brush out the tangles. I took a deep breath to soothe rattled nerves, and I was apprehensive, as I knew Chance's demeanor was too mild for the predicament we were in earlier. What would he do to me besides fuck me?

I'd learned so many carnal things in the few days we'd

been wed, but I imagined we'd only done the more innocent of acts. Chance had reassured me again and again what we did together, no matter how dirty or decadent, was beautiful. Sometimes when he was deep inside me I couldn't tell where I ended and he started. I wanted to reaffirm that now, after what we'd been through, but not knowing what he had planned made my heart rate accelerate.

"You didn't listen." A naked Chance stood in the doorway, hands up by his shoulders as he gripped the doorframe. His cock was pointed straight at me as if it knew where it wanted to be. I jumped at his words but stilled, then stared. I couldn't help it. His shoulders were broad, his belly rippled with muscle. A line of hair travelled from his navel downward into the thatch of hair at the base of his cock. I licked my lips, remembering the feel of him in my mouth, the taste of him on my tongue.

"Kitten," he prompted.

I moved into the position he wanted, my head on the pillow, my hands over my head and gripping the slats of the headboard, then looked to him. I exhaled and relaxed my tense muscles.

He hadn't moved, just followed me with his eyes. With his chin, he indicated something I forgot. Oh! My legs. I bent my knees and planted my feet on the bed, then moved them apart. Only when he was satisfied with my position did he come into the room. Putting a knee on the bed had me shifting slightly, but I remained still. Placing himself between my splayed knees, he looked his fill, taking his time. I felt his gaze on me as if it were his hand, a soft caress that had my nipples tightening and a shiver raced down my spine. My breath quickened with the anticipation and I ached for his touch. My fingers clenched nervously at the headboard, my grip slippery.

"I love you." The words came out in a blurted rush.

His eyes widened at the words, clearly surprised. I hadn't expected to say it, but I meant it.

He crooked his finger at me and I moved to sit up. A big hand snaked around my waist, pulling me into him so we were chest to chest, both on our knees atop the soft quilt. His face was so close I could see the flecks in his eyes, the whiskers on his strong jaw. I licked my lips, unsure of myself.

He groaned, then whispered, "Kitten." Lowering his head, his mouth met mine in a gentle brushing of lips. He kissed the corner of my mouth, then along my jaw until he kissed the dainty curve of my ear.

"Do you know how long I've waited for those words?" he whispered.

Another chill ran down my spine at his warm breath on my neck. He kissed my frantic pulse, then moved back up to gently suck on my earlobe.

"No," I whispered back.

"I can't remember when I didn't love you."

I froze at his words, my hands on his solid chest. "You...you do?"

"You doubt my love?" He pulled back just enough to tilt my chin up with his fingers.

"We always fight," I replied.

"I think that will change now, don't you?" He still held my chin, but his thumb ran over my lower lip.

I'd fought against everyone for so long. I couldn't

remember when I wasn't contrary. I argued just so I could be heard, which was hard when growing up in a house of ten females. So I'd found a way to have a voice and I used it often, even with Chance. I'd wanted to be free, yet I had been all along. Even Miss Trudy had alluded to it the day Chance had left for the cattle drive. Marrying Chance hadn't taken my freedom away, quite the opposite in fact. He'd given me room to be myself without the need to argue to be heard.

But I hadn't seen that. I'd continued on, arguing with a hot head and a loud mouth, fighting him just to be difficult. I'd wanted his attention, and yet I'd had it all along. *His* attention especially. Once we were married and I fought him, he'd spanked me. I didn't like it, but it had given me the attention I'd sought. It was a vicious circle that I hadn't broken from, yet Chance had seen it all along. The last time, he'd even said I'd been itching for a spanking. Most likely, I had.

"Oh." The sound slipped out.

The consequences of my flippancy had never been as extreme as on the cattle drive. It had made me learn that some boundaries couldn't be crossed, that fighting them wouldn't give me the attention I craved, but a life-threatening situation instead.

I'd put both of us in danger. I'd jeopardized the livelihood of the ranch. I remembered the booming sound of the gunshot and knew that the most precious thing in the world could have been taken away from me. And for what?

Tears welled in my throat, filled my eyes. "Oh," I repeated. "I've been so awful to you." The tears fell now, unhindered and the emotion I'd been holding inside followed with it. This was the first time I'd truly cried in...forever. "How can you say you love me when I've done nothing but fight you?"

I tilted my forehead against his chest and cried— cried for the near death we shared, for the terrible attitude I'd had with him when all he'd wanted to do was keep me safe. I cried for not appreciating Miss Trudy's words and what she'd experienced in her hard life. I'd devalued her dreams as inconsequential, when instead I should have been proud of her. She'd worked and fought incredibly hard for her dreams and all I'd done was whine.

Chance stroked my back as I sobbed, patient as always. When I was all out of tears, I hiccupped and wiped my nose with the back of my hand before he tilted my chin up once again.

"I love that you're feisty and independent and strong. Brave, too. I also like it when I get to spank you for being insolent and insubordinate and just plain cranky."

I couldn't help but give him a watery smile. "I like it when you spank me, too."

"Hmm. Then that's not much of a punishment then." He paused, the continued, "You're always with me, Rose, even when you're not there. The ride to Parsons, it was miserable. It rained."

I frowned.

"We had to sleep in the livery. Do you think I would rather be in bed with you or on hay with some horses and the other men? You may think I want to do things without you, but that's not the case. I want to be with you...always, but sometimes it's better if I'm alone."

"Because it's dangerous," I answered, my voice soft. He was explaining himself, perhaps even scolding me a little, but it didn't seem quite so harsh since we were naked and I was in his arms. I felt his cock against my belly, my breasts pressed into his chest.

"Yes, but also because I can't think clearly when you're around. You bewitch me, kitten."

The smile on my lips now was broad and genuine.

"I hated the cattle drive," I admitted. "Not just the part where a gun was waved around or I was taken away by a miserable man."

I heard a gravelly sound escape his throat, but otherwise he remained quiet.

"I didn't like the smell, or the slow pace, or falling in the creek. I hated being wet for so long. The food was terrible and it was boring."

He arched a brow.

"I was wrong."

Chance kissed my forehead, then pulled back. "I'm proud of you for admitting that, but you will be punished. Ah, kitten, the look on your face is all wrong for those words. I don't want to see eagerness, but worry instead."

I should feel contrite, but I wasn't. I felt...free. For the first time, I could release my need to be in control. I could give my body to him and I knew he'd take care of me. I didn't always have to be the one that said what was best. I backed out of Chance's hold and turned so I could lower to my forearms so my ass was in the air, presenting myself for my punishment. Looking over my shoulder, I glanced up at Chance. His hand came down on my right cheek with a loud crack, but with no force.

"You don't get to say how you will be punished, kitten. It's all up to me. Now, return to how you were instructed before, hands on the headboard."

The sting in my bottom had my nipples tightening. There was a strange connection between the twinge of pain and my arousal. I didn't say anything as I moved into the position he'd requested, hands on the headboard slats, knees bent and open.

CHANCE

"That's a good girl."

I had her exactly where I wanted her, in my bed, naked and doing my bidding. She was so receptive to my touch that getting her naked and beneath me were simple tasks. The third, her doing my bidding—well, I had hoped she would comply. Something changed while we'd been apart, in the duration when Ivers held her. Not only in me, but also in Rose as well.

I'd been forced to watch the bastard ride away with her, helpless to save her because of Stills and his fucking gun. I'd fought an armed man to rescue her and it had been worth it. My life was worthless without her. So I'd tackled the man to escape, thankful to have come away unscathed. Not only could I have been shot, but trampled as well. Both were grim demises that I refused to consider now.

When I'd been ready to save Rose from Ivers, my aid had been unnecessary. She'd been smart and used her own natural weapons, her brain and irritating way to pester someone. There was no question she was underestimated; she was a very smart woman. Even I had taken that for granted. I'd wanted to shelter her from all harm, all potential dangers, when all I'd done was put her in a makeshift prison. I'd stifled her to the point where she couldn't be herself. I had to let her make some mistakes, although her safety would never be compromised. And so I learned I needed faith, faith that Rose could defend herself, at least to a certain degree.

Rose seemed to discover something herself, that she didn't need to be so strong. She didn't need to take on the world alone. I would be there for her, helping her, supporting her from now on, and not smothering her with a blanket of overprotection as I did so. There was no question she'd argue and fight me like a wild mustang fighting a lead, but she would put value in my demands. I had reasons, and the incident with Ivers and Stills proved their worth.

Now here she was, hale and hearty, and doing my bidding. She needed to be punished for her rash actions, but a spanking wouldn't achieve the outcome I desired, for while she seemed to find it painful, it was arousing as well. I had to know, with complete certainty, that she would heed my words, that she would be contrite. A stern punishment other than spanking would ensure this would not be forgotten. And so I lowered myself between her legs, spread her thighs wide and began.

"Chance!" Rose cried as I put my mouth on her damp flesh, my tongue flat as I licked over her entire pussy. I wasn't gentle. This wasn't about her pleasure, but her punishment.

"Like that, kitten?"

I watched as her fingers whitened as she clenched the headboard. "Yes!"

"You will not come. That is your punishment."

 HANCE

I FLICKED the tip of my tongue over her little pink pearl, then stopped, stroked a finger over her slit, parting her, then teasingly circled her entrance.

"I...I don't understand," she replied breathily.

"I know your body, Rose. I know how to take you to the brink of pleasure, and then stop. Again and again."

It was punishment for me as well, for my cock ached to fill her. It wanted to feel her hot walls clench down, have the slick slide of filling her provide delicious friction. My pleasure would have to wait for I had a lesson to teach.

"This is the only way for you to know how I felt when Ivers took you. Desperate. Out of control. Angry. Insane with need."

With my mouth, I worked her into a frenzy. Feeling her clench down on the tip of my finger, I pulled back.

"No!" she cried.

I waited until she had calmed, then did it again and again until her skin was slick with sweat, her head thrashing on the pillow and tears slipped from her eyes. That was the only outlet of release I would allow her body.

"Chance, please. Oh God. I need you."

"You've got me, kitten."

She was so wet now her juices coated my chin, were slick on her thighs. Her taste would be something I'd never forget, something I would always crave.

"Are you ready to let me give you your pleasure?"

"Yes!"

"It's mine to give, isn't it, kitten?"

"Yes!"

"Who's in charge?"

"You are."

"Who will keep you safe?"

"You will."

"Who has learned you need to make some choices of your own?"

She swallowed deeply, and then looked down her body at me, confused. Her cheeks were tear stained, her face flushed, and her eyes wild with need.

"Me, kitten? This has been my punishment, too. It's torture for me to wait." I sat back on my heels and gripped the base of my cock, then stroked up the length in a firm grip. I hissed at the contact. The tip seeped clear fluid, desperate and ready to fuck. "We've both learned a lesson, haven't we?"

She nodded her head, her hair clinging to her damp brow. "Yes."

I came over her then, bracing my weight on one forearm, aligning my cock with her slick entrance. As I filled her, I kissed her. Deeply, darkly, carnally. We both groaned through the kiss as I sank in all the way. With the blunt head of my cock, I felt her womb.

She molded around me like a hand in a glove, the perfect fit. Her inner walls milked my cock as if it were trying to pull the seed from my body. She was scalding hot, tight and wet. A perfect combination I couldn't resist.

Lowering my head, I took a nipple in my mouth as I began to move. I'd been so primed that my balls had already tightened, my orgasm right there. "Come, kitten."

It didn't take more than that simple command for Rose to do as I ordered. She tensed as she cried out my name, her sweet pussy holding me tightly within as I came. My seed pulsed into her, over and over as my pleasure washed over me, so intense it was blinding. Her hands gripped my lower back, her nails digging into my flesh. She would leave marks and I would cherish them. I took a moment to catch my breath, let the last bits of pleasure course through me.

Although I'd come and come hard, I wasn't done. Far from it. My cock was ready for more and I would take it. I'd take her, for she was my wife and she was precious. She knew how much I loved her, how much I wanted her, but I'd show her as well. I'd prove it to her again and again until she would never doubt.

I pulled out, watching as my seed slipped from her, then rolled her onto her back. She sighed at the manhandling, content and sated as she was, but did not resist. There was no lingering, no additional need to arouse her as she was still highly sensitive and my cock was ready to take her again. I didn't wait, just slid into her again. She looked up at me, saw me and wrapped her legs about my waist, pulled me in closer.

"More," she whimpered. Oh yes. More.

I reached down between us and ran my finger over her clit. She was always extra sensitive after her first climax and it only took a brief amount of play for her to come a second time. She rippled and pulsed and I took this time when she was mindless to push into her further, so slick and hot around me, deeper and deeper until I was fully seated.

"There, kitten. You've taken all of me."

"You're so big. It's...I'm so full," she groaned. Her back curved and arched.

"You'll come again for me, won't you? Nothing but pleasure."

Gripping her hips, I pulled back, letting my cock work all of those pleasure spots, then filled her again. I fucked her at a slow yet deliberate pace until sweat dripped down my back. She came again, clenching me like a fist as I fucked her, and that was my undoing. I couldn't hold back my release and I slid all the way in so that I filled her deep with my seed.

Rose's entire body went slack as she breathed deeply. Slowly, I pulled free and ran my hand up and down the length of her side, wanting that continued connection while soothing her. I'd used her well, but given her pleasure. I felt virile and possessive at the sight of her sweaty and sated beneath me.

Slipping from the bed, I went to the washroom to clean myself with a cloth, then brought one back to the bedroom for Rose, who remained in the same position I left her. Although I liked to see my mark of seed on her, I gently wiped her clean. Tossing the cloth aside, I climbed in bed and pulled her in behind me. "Sleep, kitten, for you'll need it. I'm going to take you all night long."

ROSE

CHANCE DID EXACTLY as he'd said and I awoke to being taken not once, not twice, but three times. He'd been creative in the ways he fucked me, standing at the side of the bed as I lay on my back, ankles on his shoulders, on our sides as we lay like two spoons in a drawer; from behind as I knelt and gripped the headboard. I slept well past dawn and only stirred when I heard voices downstairs. Rolling over, I discovered the bed empty beside me. My body felt achy and sore, well used by Chance. It felt...good—even my bottom where he'd taken me for the first time. I wanted more. I'd become voracious for my husband and his very skilled cock.

I dressed quickly, this time donning a corset instead

of my usual wrap. Once all of the hooks had been fastened, I looked down at how my breasts were lifted. While it offered the same support to my large bosom, it did nothing to diminish it as wrapping accomplished quite successfully. Instead of grumbling about how exposed I felt, I smiled to myself, knowing Chance would be pleased. He seemed to be quite fond of my breasts and liked to give them very thorough attention. I wanted to please him first and foremost now, for when I did, he *more* than pleased me in return.

Once I'd dressed and arranged my hair into a bun, I followed the voices to the kitchen where Chance sat at the table having coffee with Miss Trudy and Hyacinth. Chance stood at my appearance and came around the table to kiss my temple. I couldn't miss the way his eyes lowered to my breasts on the way, for I knew the shape of my figure was different. "We have visitors," he commented aloud, although his eyes were telling me *"Later."*

"Yes, I can see that." I smiled wickedly, and then turned to my family. "Hello, Miss Trudy, Hyacinth." I went around the table and gave each a kiss on the cheek.

"We heard about your horrible incident from Walt."

Miss Trudy's voice was as calm as usual, but I knew she was bothered. Her lips were pinched and she gripped her mug firmly. I had amends to make, but not with the others present. She was never one to tell tales or admonish in public, therefore I knew she bided her time.

"You look quite pretty today, Rose, with that green skirt. It really complements your eyes." Hyacinth, ever the diplomat, always found something nice to say about anyone even the veritable shrews who thought lowly of the Lenox family in town. She always spoke to them without a hint of the malice I was sure she felt.

"Thank you," I said. Although she wasn't my sister by blood, she was most certainly a sister of my heart, and my favorite. While in the past I'd been bent on doing only wrong, Hyacinth was quite the opposite; I never knew her to do a misdeed in her life.

"Jackson, Big Ed's son, has arrived at the ranch," Miss Trudy said, making idle small talk.

Chance poured a cup of coffee and handed it to me as I sat beside Hyacinth. As I did so, I felt seed drip from my pussy and my eyes widened. It was warm and a surprising reminder at what I'd done with Chance just before sunrise. I looked to him, realizing his statement about being with me even when he wasn't nearby, was apt. He wasn't touching my pussy with his cock, his mouth or his fingers, but I felt him there. He watched me closely, but could not read my thoughts. If he had even an inkling, he did not let on. I just hoped I would not have a mark on my skirt, as I was not wearing any drawers.

"Really?" I asked shifting in my seat and trying to direct my thoughts away from Chance's cock. "Is Jackson an asset?"

"He is a big man and easily able to help Big Ed with the more burdensome tasks."

I glanced at Hyacinth, who fidgeted in her seat. She never did that and I was quite surprised. I even saw a flush to her cheeks.

"Do you find him acceptable, Hyacinth?" Chance

asked, leaning a hip against the sideboard. He took a sip of his coffee.

She looked down at her lap. "Yes, quite," she replied, her voice soft.

Ah. *Ah!* I glanced at Miss Trudy who smiled gently. It seemed perhaps Hyacinth had finally met her man, but if she had feelings for Big Ed's son, Miss Trudy would not speak of it and embarrass her. Hyacinth was not one to talk so openly about her feelings, unlike some of our sisters.

Hyacinth abruptly stood, her chair legs scraping on the wood floor. Chance came around quickly to pull it back for her. "Thank you," she murmured as she smoothed down her skirt. "I think it's time we left, don't you, Miss Trudy? I'm sure they are quite tired after their ordeal."

She didn't wait for the other woman to answer, just exited the room. Chance was gentleman enough to escort her outside.

Neither Miss Trudy nor I moved.

"I am quite shocked. I don't think I've ever seen Hyacinth flustered before," I said, glancing down the hall and hearing the front door close.

Miss Trudy nodded, smoothed back her already neat hair. "Yes, Jackson is a very handsome man. All of the girls have been making calf eyes at him, but to no avail. Hyacinth has been avoiding the man, as is her norm, but he seems quite taken by her. It is amusing to watch."

"Miss Trudy," I began, wanting to direct the conversation away from Hyacinth's romantic interests.

She held up her hand. "I am glad you are well."

It was my turn to glance at my lap, but I did not fixate there. I lifted my chin and looked her square in the eye. "I owe you an apology for leaving as I did. I was impulsive and reckless and caused you fear unnecessarily."

"You are in love," she replied with a small shrug.

I nodded without hesitation. "Yes, yes I am. But that's no excuse for my behavior. What you shared with me was not understood until yesterday. I admire your bravery and am appreciative of what you've done for all of us."

I saw her in a completely new light now. Perhaps it was because I'd grown up in the very short time since I married Chance, or learned some things, even outside of the bedroom. It had been six days, but I saw the world differently, saw people differently. I'd gained the perspective only marriage could provide, and it made me perhaps a little more empathetic, or at least I hoped so.

"Love changes a person, Rose. For me, it was you and your sisters. For you, perhaps you will be blessed with children of your own, but I am glad to see you finally discover your feelings for Chance. He has always been the man for you. I knew it all along, but it was to happen in your time, not mine." She smiled a little slyly. "Although I think Chance may have nudged you along."

I thought about the seed that made my thighs damp. Every time we came together, Chance's seed had been copious, our lovemaking ardent and frequent. He was correct; I could be with child. It was one task on the ranch that only I could fulfill, and while he put exceptionally good effort into the creation, I was to be the nurturer, the life giver. Or, I could look at it not as a task, but as the one thing, the only thing, that Chance and I would create that was completely both of ours.

"Yes, I think perhaps he did."

Miss Trudy stood. I followed suit.

She came around the table, put her hands on my shoulders. "Out of all my girls, you have always been the sensible one, thinking of tangible things while the others had their minds in the clouds. They talk about ribbons and lace to no end. Perhaps now it's time for the roles to be reversed, although I do not foresee any lace on any of your bodices. Let go, Rose. Enjoy life. Let Chance take some of your burdens, for he is strong enough to do it."

CHANCE PULLED ME INTO HIM, my back to his front, as we watched Miss Trudy and Hyacinth ride away.

"I'm surprised they're riding the wagon," I commented.

Chance kissed the top of my head. "If Jackson is as keen on Hyacinth as it seems, then I'm sure he did it so he could help her down on her return."

The idea had merit, for Hyacinth could not turn down the man's aid. I turned in the circle of Chance's arms so I could look at him. "That's devious planning. Is that what men really do?"

"To what, get to put their hands on a woman?"

"There's nothing inappropriate about what Jackson would do, is there?" My worry for Hyacinth's virtue must have shown on my face.

"I'm sure Jackson is a perfect gentleman. To ease your

mind, we will visit tomorrow. I would like to get a glimpse of this man myself."

I arched a brow. "Now who's the protective one?"

"She is my sister now," Chance replied, his voice hinting at his protective nature.

"Tomorrow then. In the meantime, I wanted to try something Miss Trudy mentioned."

Chance's brows went up beneath his hair. "Oh?"

"She said because you are so strong, I should let you take on some of my burdens."

He ran the back of his knuckles over my cheek. "I assume she was not speaking entirely of physical burdens."

I shook my head slowly. "No. I don't believe so."

"What are you implying, kitten?"

I smiled mischievously as I ran my hands over his chest. "I thought I'd allow you to have your way with me."

Chance froze. "Allow me? Every time we fuck I take control."

I glanced up at him through my lashes. "Except that one time." I flushed at what I'd done.

"Kitten, I *allowed* you to take control," he countered.

I felt cranky all of a sudden. "Very well. Then this time when we fuck, you may do whatever you want." My tone was a little tart. This was not going as I'd planned.

"Hey there. Shh," he crooned. "You're being serious and I was poking fun. Tell me, kitten. I want to hear."

"I want to let go, Chance. To truly give myself to you and know that you'll keep me safe."

He hissed out a breath as he tilted my chin up. I met his dark gaze. I saw everything there—his heart, his love, his very soul. "I'll keep you safe, kitten." He took my hand, his big and warm and gentle. "Come."

He pulled me not in the direction of the house, but toward the stable. "Where are we going?"

"I need some rope for what I'm going to do to you."

My feet skidded across the ground as my pace slowed while his was still insistent. "Rope?"

He looked back over his shoulder at me and I caught my breath. This man, this handsome, virile, arousing man, was mine. "Aren't you supposed to be compliant sometimes? Let go, kitten. I'll keep you safe."

He repeated the words again, like a mantra. I quickened my pace and followed him, not only so he could have his decadent and most likely tawdry way with me, but letting him lead me through whatever life would bring.

Ready for more Lenox Ranch Cowboys? Click here to read Spurs & Satin!

Unlocking Hyacinth's heart will mean a battle of wills, but love is worth the fight.

When handsome soldier Jackson Reed returns home from the Army, one woman catches his eye. She notices him as well but why is she doing everything she can to avoid him? Hyacinth Lenox can't stop thinking about Jackson Reed, she wants him but she can't have him. Guild from a tragic childhood incident follows her everywhere and she feels undeserving of Jackson's love. He's a man who gets what he wants...and he wants Hyacinth.

Don't miss the second book in the Lenox Ranch Cowboys series with a shy heroine and obsessed war hero determined to make her his.

Click here to read <u>Spurs & Satin</u> now!

JOIN THE WAGON TRAIN!

If you're on Facebook, please join my closed group, the Wagon Train! Don't miss out on the giveaways and hot cowboys!

https://www.facebook.com/groups/vanessavalewagontrain/

GET A FREE BOOK!

Join my mailing list to be the first to know of new releases, free books, special prices and other author giveaways.

http://freeromanceread.com

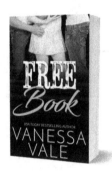

ALSO BY VANESSA VALE

Wild Mountain Men

Mountain Darkness

Mountain Delights

Mountain Desire

Mountain Danger

Grade-A Beefcakes

Sir Loin Of Beef

T-Bone

Tri-Tip

Porterhouse

Skirt Steak

Small Town Romance

Montana Fire

Montana Ice

Montana Heat

Montana Wild

Montana Mine

Steele Ranch

Spurred

Wrangled

Tangled

Hitched

Lassoed

Bridgewater County

Ride Me Dirty

Claim Me Hard

Take Me Fast

Hold Me Close

Make Me Yours

Kiss Me Crazy

Mail Order Bride of Slate Springs

A Wanton Woman

A Wild Woman

A Wicked Woman

Bridgewater Brides

Their Runaway Bride

Their Kidnapped Bride

Their Wayward Bride

Their Captivated Bride

Their Treasured Bride

Their Christmas Bride

Their Reluctant Bride

Their Stolen Bride

Their Brazen Bride

Their Rebellious Bride

Their Reckless Bride

Outlaw Brides

Flirting With The Law

MMA Fighter Romance

Fight For Her

Lenox Ranch Cowboys

Cowboys & Kisses

Spurs & Satin

Reins & Ribbons

Brands & Bows

Lassos & Lace

Montana Men

The Lawman

The Cowboy

The Outlaw

Standalone Reads

Twice As Delicious

Western Widows

Sweet Justice

Mine To Take

Relentless

Sleepless Night

Man Candy - A Coloring Book

ABOUT THE AUTHOR

Vanessa Vale is the *USA Today* bestselling author of sexy romance novels, including her popular Bridgewater historical series and hot contemporary romances. With over one million books sold, Vanessa writes about unapologetic bad boys who don't just fall in love, they fall hard. Her books are available worldwide in multiple languages in e-book, print, audio and even as an online game. When she's not writing, Vanessa savors the insanity of raising two boys and figuring out how many meals she can make with a pressure cooker. While she's not as skilled at social media as her kids, she loves to interact with readers.

BookBub

Instagram

www.vanessavaleauthor.com

CPSIA information can be obtained
at www.ICGtesting.com
Printed in the USA
LVHW010317170322
713569LV00016B/2226